TOWN TRAP

DR. CARTER BROWN

CONTENTS

JD Books are published by

JD Publishing Company
#3-422, 4TH STREET
Estevan, Saskatchewan
S4A 0V1 Canada

A special thank you goes out to Jibril Shaban, Professor Rudolf Zawaski, Willian Vansac and John Attrel for your support. I also want to thank my editors, and my design team, including my wonderful family for always being there

Little Wizard

A warm breeze drifting through Michael's room hummed softly in his ears as he awoke, full of energy at Thorn Valley Camp. Michael bathed and dressed sharply in his official uniform: a sky-blue, long-sleeved shirt, navy-blue necktie, pants, coat, and shiny black shoes. As he ambled from the compound, his eyes suddenly brightened at the sight of a thirteen-year-old boy with a spotless, round face and blue eyes walking toward him.

"Hello, my name is Lee Bilondov. I arrived last night from Flomoville. I am a regular here. How about you? What is your name?"

"Michael. I am from Handii, and this is my first time."

"Why are you kept in a separate bunk?"

"Maybe they think I'm special." Michael laughed, hoping Lee wouldn't pick up that he was King Flomo's son. Whenever Michael left the palace in Livingstone, he would enter the Hot Room near his bedroom where he would bathe in special waters. The heated water changed his fair hair and hazel eyes to the color of whatever button he pressed on the wall. But since Thorn Valley was so far from home, Michael didn't bother with the Hot Room.

"Friends?" Lee shook his hand.

"Sure! Why not?"

"Come," Lee said. "I'll show you around and introduce you to some of my friends."

Michael, an unsuspecting twelve-year-old, followed his new friend's lead.

Thorn Valley Camp was situated over one hundred miles from Handii, the capital city of the Kingdom of Livingstone. Huge and exhilarating, Thorn Valley hosted 147 other children that summer, budding young wizards from around the kingdom eager to bolster their magic skills and acquire new tricks. The University of Flomoville, the third largest in the province, sponsored the program.

Lee kicked his heels in the soft earth as they walked toward a crowd of young wizards who were performing magic tricks. Mioexfo Stonedell, an eleven-year-old boy, stood in the middle of a crowd of onlookers. He took off his right shoe and held it up in the air for everyone to see; then, in an instant, he transformed it into a box. The crowd roared with delight at the spectacle.

"Do you want to take a look? Come, let's watch," Lee said. "Magic is everywhere."

"Are you a magician, too?" Michael asked.

"No, but I'd like to be."

Mioexfo sauntered over to Michael, who stood to the right of the crowd and implored him for his left shoestring.

"Why?"

"Just do it," Lee insisted.

Despite his apprehension, Michael bent down to remove the black shoestring from his left shoe. He handed it to Mioexfo, who passed it around for examination. After it made its way back to Mioexfo, he dashed it to the solid ground. Suddenly, it transmogrified into a baby goanna, who sprung to life in a burst of confusion, crying and running around. Michael froze; the wonder of what he just witnessed dazzled him.

Mioexfo caught the goanna, altered it back into Michael's shoestring, and returned it with a grin. Michael nervously viewed it before slipping it into his front right pocket. The crowd dispersed.

"Where can I see this magician perform again?" Michael asked.

"I don't know. He arrived this morning, and it's my first time seeing him. He was pretty good, wasn't he?"

"For sure! I love magic, and it's my dream to become a magician like him some day."

"It's time for breakfast," Lee reminded him as they trudged down to the large cafeteria, already exuding the alluring scent of syrupy waffles and rich sausages. The campers heaped food on their trays and took their seats, eager to eat. Lee stood on the table and clanged a spoon against a teacup to capture the attention of the room.

"Attention, attention! I present to you Thorn Valley's newest member!"

Michael stood up and said, "I'm overjoyed to be here, and I want to know each of you by names."

Right after breakfast, the crowd gathered around him to introduce themselves, and Michael silently strained to memorize each of their names. He made many friends that day, the rest of which was dedicated to a compelling horse hockey match from which Michael's team emerged the narrow victors.

That night, Michael fell into his bed very tired. But only two hours later, his peaceful slumber was interrupted by the odor of rancid breath and the sensation of something soft licking his face. As he sluggishly opened his eyes, he was shocked to see a massive, hairy, black mountain gorilla staring into his face. The creature stood six feet tall, revealing its imposing build—long, muscular arms, massive chest, and broad hands and feet. Standing upright, it glared pugnaciously at Michael before lunging madly to bite his face, narrowly missing as Michael turned his body and fell from the bed.

Michael jumped to his feet, screaming loudly to scare off the gorilla, but it savagely roared and pounded its chest, hurling the lamp stand at Michael as it moved to grab him. Michael raced through the door, with the gorilla in ferocious, determined pursuit.

Thorn Valley was unsettlingly quiet. Michael wondered if anyone could hear his voice as he screamed. The gorilla chased him, running on his knuckles in close pursuit. As Michael glanced behind, the gorilla viciously sprung toward him, and, unable to outrun the beast and screaming wildly, Michael slid into a crouch, covering his face as he braced himself for the intense pain.

"Why are you yelling, young man? Are you all right?" a deep, muffled voice suddenly asked him.

He opened his eyes and saw a lavishly dressed old man standing above him, offering his right hand to help him up. Without speaking, Michael extended his left hand, and the man yanked him to his feet.

"Where did it go?" he gasped, finding nothing in sight but the sleepy town and the inky night sky.

"I certainly don't know what you are talking about. I didn't see anything. I only heard you yelling, failing to realize that others are sleeping," the man, a tall, chubby sixty-nine-year-old with bushy, long white hair and a bushy, white beard, answered authoritatively. "My name is Professor Leo Oden. I am the assistant coordinator to Professor James Barclay, and you are Michael Blackwell. I have been expecting you. I hope you like it here. Now go to bed, and I'll see you first thing in the morning."

"Sir, please," Michael pleaded. "I can't sleep in that room, because I saw my belt transmuting into a bunch of wild scorpions earlier, and I was only able to save myself by hurling them out the window. And just now, I had a terrifying encounter with a big, frightening ape that nearly broke me into pieces. I am so scared. It's better to sleep out here."

Leo Oden said nothing but nodded with an air of understanding. He led Michael to his master suite, an impregnable chamber closely watched over by his loyal guards. Michael looked around the large bedroom in the wooden cabin. His eyes were drawn almost immediately to a large photograph dominating the wall over the bed: a portrait of Leo Oden and Professor Barclay shaking hands.

"I think you'll remain unscathed here. Good night." He gently closed the door and went to Professor Barclay's office. Leo Oden knew that the professor would be in his office, as his entire staff had just concluded a late-night meeting in the adjacent chamber room. Since most of the teachers were wizards and sorcerers, they were told to keep students' expectations high and encourage them to work harder on their various magical skills.

Leo Oden entered the office, a luxurious room appointed with locally crafted mahogany furniture. "The King's son is scared. Says he saw some terrifying things," Leo Oden told Professor Barclay.

The professor smirked malevolently. "Now I have him right in my trap, just as I planned. I will take my revenge on that rat for all the atrocities his father inflicted on me," Professor Barclay said, rubbing his gray beard. Towering over six feet, the professor had, even at seventy, a set of bright, large, white teeth that showed through his crafty grin.

"That's insane, Professor. He's a good kid. Remember, only Michael knows the secret code of his father's powers, and the almighty spirits of this kingdom are protecting him. If you go after him, you may get yourself killed. You cannot kill his father without killing him first, and if you kill him, we may never get the secret code."

"He's just like his wicked father, whom I will never forgive. I have been seeking vengeance that will bring about the death of his father, and this is the perfect time! I must find a way to get that secret code and use it against him and his father."

"Why are you so angry with them?"

"Leo, my real name is Egbash Blackwell."

Leo gasped. "You are related?"

"I am Michael's uncle, his father's fraternal twin brother."

Leo was taken aback. "So why do you want to kill them?"

"Fifty-eight years ago, his virulent father stole my birthright—my pride and glory, the throne of Livingstone. I was the favorite son of my father, who wanted me to become the next king. Michael's selfish father cruelly poisoned both my father and me. Michael's grandfather died painfully, but my servants secretly slipped me out of the palace and took me to Flomoville, the third largest province in the kingdom where I was in a coma for a year. I changed my name and disguised my identity. Six years later, one of the servants who had spirited me out of the palace was captured and brutally tortured by the king's men before he confessed that I had survived the poisoning.

"Michael's father has wrathfully hunted me for almost twenty-three years. This is the first time I have told a soul. Soon, my plan will succeed. I will emerge out of my iron cage to gain what is rightfully mine." Professor Barclay swiveled around in his chair. His eyes were cast in a furious glare.

"You are the mightiest sorcerer the universe has ever known," Leo Oden said, realizing that with his staff of wizards and magicians, Professor Barclay had the power to destroy people and level entire towns. Terror gripped him. "I promise to help you. We should follow him from now on until we discover the best possible opportunity to kill him."

Professor Barclay rose to his feet and embraced him as they chuckled nefariously. "Thank you."

* * * * *

Earlier, Michael had met with Montgomery Wandom, the chief spiritual adviser of Livingstone. In keeping with tradition and in preparation for his future role as king, Michael was sent to Professor James Barclay at Thorn Valley to perfect his magic on a secret epic journey to unknown land. If he returned successfully, Professor Wandom informed him, the spiritual committee of Livingstone would grant him a personal protection code upon his succession to the throne. This code, a sacred secret guarded closely by Livingstone's royal order, was a six-character, proto-Sinitic alphabetical symbol carefully selected to represent the meaning of Michael's name, the Lion-Eyeball. Only to be activated when he was king, it would bestow upon him ultimate powers over his enemies.

* * * * *

The following morning, right after breakfast, Professor Barclay gathered all the campers in the auditorium. After welcoming them, he dispersed them to explore their neatly landscaped camp, which stored many arcane hidden treasures. Professor Barclay and Leo Oden secretly watched Michael as they began planning how they would destroy him.

Michael and Lee took their notebooks and decamped to the east. They stumbled across a large, deep pond, a stretch of watery black mud covered with dry brown leaves that had fallen from the trees.

"We must go across," Lee said, walking in front.

As he approached the dark water, Michael suddenly slipped, reaching out instinctively at Lee's shirt for balance, and both of them tumbled into the murky water. With the brown leaves swirling around their submerged bodies, they managed to swim to the other side but emerged soaked, uncomfortable, and covered in the stench of the black mud. They were embarrassed to return with the dark mud covering their bodies.

"We have to find a place to clean up, but I think we're lost; there's no road here," Michael said. Scanning the landscape, he drew Lee's attention to a sweeping, open valley in the distance on the other side of the forest. "We should search down the valley for clean, fresh water."

They trudged through the grassy stretch, pushing away tall leaves and untamed brush as they struggled to navigate through the woods. After trekking for ten minutes through the verdant tangle of bushes and trees, Lee suddenly stopped; it was dead silent. Michael thought he saw something frightening, so he stood quietly, carefully listening and inspecting the grounds.

"Let's make our way through the hard green bush on the left." Lee said, taking a long, dry branch and beating through the vegetation while Michael followed.

They had walked for a long stretch down the hill when Michael stopped and asked Lee, "Do you know this place well?"

"Don't be scared; just follow me because we're almost there." After a few minutes, Michael heard a waterfall. He stared at Lee. When they got to the water, it flowed with a rapid current down the deep valley.

"I think we should keep walking down," Michael said.

"Okay."

They continued downhill until they came to a wide river with a rough current rushing at a pace they hadn't seen before.

"Wait, Michael! This isn't normal water."

"You're the one who brought us here, so you have to figure something out. I really need a bath!"

"So now you're blaming me? We were searching for water, and I brought you to some. You should be thanking me!"

"I'm not blaming you! I just thought that you were knowledge-able enough about this camp to find a solution!"

Lee turned to the river as Michael moved back and sat on a big black rock, waiting for him to decide what to do next.

The perilously swift current frightened Michael as he observed it from his perch on the rock. If they washed themselves, would the current take them downstream? As he watched, Lee dipped his right hand into the water to investigate. He screamed and jerked back his hand, clutching it in excruciating pain. The water felt hard as ice and almost broke his fingers. He ran back to Michael.

"That water is alive! Do you think there's other water around here?" Michael asked.

"I don't think so. We must figure out a way to use it. Can you remember what Professor Barclay told us? He said that the human brain is smarter than modern-day computers and that nothing is impossible. I want us to use our brains and make this work for us," Lee said.

"You're right. Come, let's try," Michael said.

Michael stared at the clear water and tried to touch it, but it grabbed his right hand like glue. When he pulled his hand out, it was sticky. But when Lee touched the water, it felt hard and cold like ice.

"I think we have different body mechanisms. This is why we're getting different reactions from this water. Besides, we aren't even sure if this is real," Michael noted.

"What do you mean?"

"I mean this water isn't real, simple as that. It's something else— like a death trap." Then, in a flash, they found themselves standing in the middle of the river on a tiny island.

The clear blue water slowly began to close in on them. They panicked, unsure of what to do and eyeing with fear the creeping water line. Within minutes, the water expanded upwards, as if made of solid material, reaching the height of a mountain and trapping them beneath the imposing height of its watery walls. It was so high they couldn't see the top. Various types of fish and aquatic plant life remained visible in the massive, liquid mountain.

"Oh my, we're about to die!" Michael yelled. They trembled as they held each other tightly, trying not to move or touch the water.

"I thought we were on the mainland. What happened?" Michael asked. He shook with fear. "I don't know. What have we done to deserve this?"

"This couldn't be one of Professor Wandom's tests, could it?"

"Look!" Michael said. "I can't turn. I might step in this water, and if I do, something might happen again."

But they had no way to turn without touching the water, whose threat was compounded by the brutal wind, which whipped around their hair every direction.

"Please listen to me," Michael pleaded. "Since we're about to die, I want you to help me scream out my parents' names. We'll start with my mother, Queen Bindu, and then my father, King Flomo Blackwell."

Lee froze as he looked disbelievingly at Michael, and the gravity of what Michael just said dawned on him. "Are you the real prince of Livingstone?"

"There's no time for answers; we're going to die anyway!" Michael said.

Michael counted to three, and they both screamed out the names loudly. After a couple of seconds, their voices echoed, repeating the names in a sharp voice.

When nothing happened, Michael screamed, "What are you waiting for? Come and kill us!"

"Shut up! What do you think you're doing?" Lee screamed at him.

"Don't tell me to shut up! We've been standing here far too long now, and I'm sick and tired of this silly water!"

They stood there for two hours, hoping the water would return to its original form while trying to twist and turn, but at that moment, the water's color transformed to dark blue.

"I knew there was something about this water when I first saw it. I'm so sorry for bringing you here. If we die, it's my fault!" Lee cried.

"No, it isn't your fault! You did what you could."

"If you are the prince of Livingstone, why doesn't anyone in town know about it?"

"I like to keep it a secret."

"Why?"

"False respect."

"Huh?"

"When people know I am a prince, they treat me with false respect. I want to be respected for being Michael, not Prince Blackwell."

"Who cares? If they had known, we might not have been in this predicament right now."

Lee then carefully tried to step on the water, but this time, as if it was real water, it dampened his shoe. He asked Michael to do the same, and the same thing happened.

"Actually, this is the first time I saw water that stands up this high and has such a mystical color," Michael said.

"I think there are myths or strong spiritual forces behind this."

"You're right," Michael repeated.

As they pondered the mystery of the water, they heard a sweet, silky female voice singing through the wind, softly intoning, "You're correct, there is. Some people define a magician as one who seeks to control, even with a mysterious power. But I define it as someone who performs an act that is unbelievably hard to describe. To become a magician you must be strong mentally and believe that everything is possible. When you want things to be done, they will be done." Maybe this *was* one of Professor Wandom's tests.

When the voice died down, a mighty wind started to blow from above as they embraced each other tightly. The wind jostled the water like a mighty ice block, and the water started splitting as it turned into an upright ice slab like a big, shiny glass door.

A stunningly attractive woman emerged from a door in the ice. Dressed in a long, white dress that covered her arms and legs, she grinned and curtsied.

"My name is Azamerie Vzixobe," she said, addressing them by their names, and invited them inside.

Azamerie Vzixobe appeared to be six feet tall, taller than Michael and Lee. She was slim, and her blonde hair flowed below her waist. Her green eyes had a distant look. Michael guessed her age at no more than twenty-six.

Lee started to follow her, but Michael quickly pulled him back.

"I believe she's a sorceress," he whispered.

She heard it and turned. "If I was, I could have killed you a long time ago."

She pointed her right hand at them, and they noticed that their wet and muddy clothes had changed into new, pristine white suits.

"If you want to live, you'd better follow me right now, because once I enter I can't come out. This water will plaster and destroy anything that doesn't belong inside. I mean *anything*—like the two of you," she said as she turned and walked through the door.

Lee gave Michael a frightened look, and then they ran to catch up with her before the large ice door slammed shut after them.

The Sorceress of Texdulonicram

They walked down a spotless wide staircase for twenty minutes before entering a beautiful house crammed with glamorous women. The women were all so gorgeous; Michael and Lee didn't know which one to stare at, as they were all indistinguishable and their inexplicable identicalness confused the pair. They quickly lost Azamerie but managed to find an exit out of the house. Stumbling through the doorway, they stood on the cusp of a prosperous and vibrant city crammed with stunning women.

"Look, Michael, we can't tell who is who. They are interchangeable, and Azamerie has vanished among them."

"Well, I think we should just keep walking. Maybe we'll find her someplace."

"Are you out of your mind? We could never tell if it was her even if we did see her."

"There must be something that distinguishes them," Michael said.

"Good luck," replied Lee sarcastically.

The cityscape was adorned with multitudes of skyscrapers and fancifully shaped houses. The people passed without noticing them. Even the roads were dotted with stunning luxury vehicles—something they hadn't seen too often in Livingstone.

"Look how big everything is," Lee said, squinting upwards at the tall buildings.

"I don't know what kind of city this is, but they are far more advanced," Michael said.

"I think we should ask somebody for help," Lee suggested.

"Excuse me." Michael stopped one of the pedestrians. He introduced Lee and himself and then explained their predicament. She patiently listened and then explained, "The name of this kingdom is Texdulonicram, and the name of this city is Kshuludiom." She told them she wasn't sure where Thorn Valley was, nor did she know how to get there. Then she walked away.

They spotted a restaurant full of people gathered in little groups, eating strange, unfamiliar dishes and speaking in an accent.

"Since we've been here, I haven't seen any men yet. Are we the only men in this entire city? How come no woman is paying attention to us? I think if they did realize our gender, they all might want a piece of us." Michael laughed.

"I'm hungry; how about you?"

"Me too; let's go eat with these women," Michael said.

They went into the restaurant and took some food off the counter. Then they sat down on the floor to eat, but the taste was unappealing. Eager for something more palatable, they decided to taste every one of the cooked dishes. The employees stood patiently watching them, and then began to wonder why they looked strange; they hadn't seen anyone in such form before—not in a long time.

Finally, Michael and Lee found what they were searching for: spicy baked chicken. They stuffed themselves while the women gathered to watch how they ate. After they finished, they returned the plates and bestowed compliments on the staff. As they walked out, the cashier called them politely and presented the bill.

"Pay with what?" Michael asked in surprise.

"Pay with money, aliens!" she answered rudely.

"I'm sorry; we thought the food was free. Honestly, we don't have money," Michael said.

"I don't know what planet you've dropped from, but you must pay. Look what you've done—you gulped down all of my baked chickens!"

"Was that really a chicken?" Lee grinned innocently.

"Don't play with me, aliens!" she warned them aggressively.

"It was delicious!" he said again.

The woman rang a bell for help. Two huge, fearsome, muscular women tramped toward them and asked if there was a problem.

Michael and Lee tried to bolt, but the women guarding the first glass door ensnared them in their grasp and grappled with them until the two giant women arrived. They whacked them soundly and tossed them into a room at the back of their restaurant, where they were told they would remain until they could come up with a concrete payment plan.

"These ladies are very cruel," Lee said.

"They're angry; I thought the food was free. We made a faux pas. We should've asked before eating. I think we're in trouble."

"Maybe we could ask for Azamerie to help us," Lee suggested.

A few minutes later, the rugged women opened the door and brusquely threw a broom and a mop at them, commanding them to sweep and shine the entire restaurant. Only then could they go free.

"Tell them who you are," Lee pleaded.

"No, I am not allowed," Michael replied, picking up the broom and beginning to sweep.

"Why?"

"You are the only one who knows who I am, and that's the way it has to be."

"You know what? I think you're making it up."

"What?"

"You are. Because you couldn't save us when you called out the king and queen's names. If you were really a prince, you would be able to save us. I don't believe you," Lee muttered, watching Michael work.

"Fine, think what you want. Let's just get to work cleaning up this place so we can find a way to get back to Thorn Valley." Michael swept furiously and in silence, eager to finish.

The women kept vigil as they completed their tasks; their stern eyes followed the pair as they moved back and forth across the floor. The women firmly warned them that they should ask before touching anything. "Nothing in this land is free," said the tallest. She also told the boys to leave and never return. "If we ever see you again, you will be exterminated."

"Yes, we understand, and we'll be leaving shortly, but a woman by the name of Azamerie brought us to this land and then vanished, leaving us all by ourselves. Do you know where we might be able to find her?" Michael asked softly.

"How do you know her?" one of the giant women asked. At that moment, Michael and Lee's eyes blinked from side to side.

"She's our good friend," Lee said.

When the women heard this, they fled like innocent deer escaping ravenous lions. Michael and Lee didn't understand why. They hadn't told them where they might find Azamerie. Michael and Lee dashed out of the restaurant quickly and ran across the street, while the women vanished in the bustling crowd. Michael stood for a moment and glanced around.

"Let's get away from this vicinity," he said. They walked toward the west where the buildings became sparse. The sun reflected from one of the silver buildings, forcing Michael to block its harsh glare with his palm.

* * * * *

"Fools! Fools!" Professor Barclay snarled. "Did you see how they expected to get all that food for nothing? A chip off the old block, that Michael, just like his dad; he takes what doesn't belong to him." Professor Barclay sat behind his mahogany desk with his legs on the table. "Don't forget what I told you, Azamerie; I want the code and then I want him dead. Is that clear?"

Azamerie watched him from her foot-to-ceiling screen carefully. "Clear, Professor. We are following the plan to the letter."

* * * * *

A woman dressed in a black suit and black high-heeled shoes pursued Michael and Lee. It appeared as if she were singing to herself. Lee noticed her and pinched Michael in an effort to make him look. They stopped, pretending they had misplaced something and were searching for it.

When they looked up, they spotted her at a distance, but in that moment, she swiftly disappeared. Suddenly, they saw her across the street opposite them again. While their eyes were still glued on her, she started disappearing and swiftly reappearing. Finally, she materialized directly at their feet.

"Hello there! My name is Azameraly Wasawaluv, and I'm the special assistant to Azamerie. She has sent me to get you."

"How do we know Azamerie actually sent you? You just heard that we were looking for her," Michael said with skepticism as Lee looked on in agreement.

"I know who you are in Livingstone and who you are going to become. I was there when Azamerie brought you here." Michael didn't believe her. Noting his incredulity, she began relating stories about their past. She told Lee that he stood in line forever at the school cafeteria at lunch for a bite to eat, while several of Michael's friends waited on him hand and foot. She told Lee he had to beg his friends to hold his backpack for just one moment, when Michael's friends begged for an opportunity to hold his. She told Lee that he would always get into trouble with the teachers for the most minor things, while Michael's teachers lavished him with praise and presented him as an example to the class.

"That sucks. So I guess you are a prince. Should I bow or something?" Lee asked his friend, who jostled him in the arm.

"What I'd like to know is how she knows so much," Michael whispered in Lee's ear.

"I've been following you all day, giving you the opportunity to explore our wonderful city and see the power of women. We cherish beauty, so we work hard to create it."

"Actually, this kingdom is delightful. I haven't seen any place like it before. One day, I would like my kingdom to have the luxuries you have here. And I admire your knowledge." Michael complimented her.

"Thank you," she said. "Let's go." Within seconds, they were standing in the presence of Azamerie, who sat in the middle of other glamorous females. Every item in her palace shone white and all her servants were adorned in crisp, clean white robes.

She approached them. "Welcome to my kingdom of Texdulonicram. I hope you enjoyed your little tour of Kshuludiom," she said with a grin. "Did you find it difficult locating my palace? I understand you were looking for me."

"We don't even understand how we got here," Michael answered.

"Come with me."

They followed her into a large empty room. "You see this huge wall? This is where I was watching you today." She stared at the white wall. Laser-like red lights shot from her eyes and penetrated the white wall, which gyrated into a big screen. "I can watch my entire kingdom from here. Your kingdom is far behind in technology," she told Michael, laughing cunningly.

"I have seen places similar to this before," Michael noted after agreeing.

"Sure you have, but the purpose for which I called you here today is because I understand you want to become a magician. We love magic in this city. Tomorrow, there will be a magic competition at our city center stadium. I've booked you two as partakers."

"What? You want us to compete?" Michael watched Azamerie lift one side of her white robe as she walked closer to him.

"As you can see, our people haven't seen men. They might worship you if you do well." She tapped Michael on the shoulder.

"We're not magicians. We got lost at Thorn Valley when we went out to explore the grounds," Michael said, and Lee nodded in agreement. "All of a sudden, we found ourselves here. Please, if you could just give us directions back to Thorn Valley, we would be so grateful."

Azamerie watched them skillfully. "I can see you boys are exhausted and need some rest." She called two of her most reliable servants and asked them to find the boys a room in the palace so they could sleep.

"No, wait! We won't leave your sight unless you tell us who you are and what kind of city this is, including everything we must know!" Lee boldly demanded.

"You're a brave young man. No woman in my kingdom has ever been plucky enough to demand such a thing of Azamerie as you just did," she smiled.

"How would they when they believe you're a god? I'm sure if you had men around here they would talk to you the same way!" Michael added.

"You seem not to realize that you are in my territory now. I make the rules and ask the questions around here. I'm the great Azamerie, ruler and creator of Texdulonicram! I created everything that survives in this land to worship only me. If they don't, death is their punishment.

"I'm two million years old. I can do anything I want and travel anywhere I want. I already took your magic powers before allowing you into my kingdom. Since you're here, you will do as I command, or you will be punished equally as the others. I will treat you no differently from my people.

"Normally, people who enter this land through that door immediately transmogrify into a female, no matter how powerful they are magically. You thought you saw water, but you failed to realize it was my trap. Most people you see here fell into it just like you, and I fished them into my kingdom." Azamerie laughed uproariously.

"I didn't change you two into females because you are a prince and Lee is your friend, but this doesn't mean I can't destroy you. I will give your magic powers tomorrow, but only when you've decided to partake in my competition."

"Why can't you give it to us at this minute? Are you scared?" Michael asked.

"I'm not afraid of anyone! I wasn't talking to you, by the way, because you have no powers—only a big mouth. I was speaking to Lee."

"How can you be a leader when everybody is scared of your name?" Michael asked.

"That's how it should be. As a leader, my people must obey me and know their parameters. You have only one life, and you must not risk it."

"No! I don't want to be that kind of ruler," Michael promptly said, glaring at Azamerie.

"Who knows if you will be a ruler?" Her laughter echoed through the large palace. "I think it's time for you to have some rest, because tomorrow will be epic. I'll see you in the morning." And with that, she vanished.

Azamerie's aides ushered Michael and Lee into their room and wished them good night before leaving them alone. The exotic furnishings and lush décor of the room stirred their excitement. It was spacious and richly decorated with white furniture. Two white beds were adorned with criss-crossed swords on either side. White bulbs bobbed up and down from the ceiling. A cold air swept through the room, lulling them into a deep, sound sleep.

* * * * *

In the screen room, Azamerie draped herself with her robe as she sat on a white lounge sofa. "Professor Barclay! Professor Barclay!"

"What is it, Azamerie?"

"Let me have them as slaves forever."

"What are you saying, Azamerie? I need my code."

"If I get you the code, will you let me have them as slaves?"

"Get the code first," Professor Barclay roared, and Azamerie shut the screen with the remote.

* * * * *

Early the next morning, Michael and Lee freshened up and got dressed. They ambled to the breakfast table where women served them and indulged their appetite to their satisfaction.

"They are treating us like kings," Lee whispered to Michael.

"Shut up! We should think about the reason behind this. I had a bad dream, and I woke up angry this morning!"

"Don't be silly; she's very nice. Can't you understand, she knows all about you and she wants us to be her friend? Maybe she thinks she will need help from you in the future when you're king. As for me, I will relish every moment, starting with this; you may join me if you want." Lee lifted up a honey-glazed croissant and licked it audibly. Michael stared at him and kept quiet.

Azamerie appeared, greeted them, and sat in front of them.

"How was your night?"

"It was one of our best nights ever," Lee answered, which excited Azamerie, who smiled widely.

Magical Mix-up

"You must now consider your magical capabilities, because today you'll be vying against other great magicians," Azamerie announced. "This competition will offer great rewards that will reconstruct your lives, I guarantee you that. You have five hours; I'll send my special assistant to fetch you and bring you to where I'll be. Have fun!" Azamerie grinned as she disappeared.

Michael and Lee glanced around and noticed that the big dining room had become empty. Everyone had vanished. The white, padded seats Michael and Lee sat on suddenly vibrated violently and threw them into the walls, almost breaking their noses.

They sat on the floor watching the two seats move along with the others, gather in the middle of the room, and suddenly drop under the floor. The floor quickly plastered back to normal as if nothing had happened. Michael and Lee were now in an open, empty room; it was a sign of the potent power of Azamerie.

Michael stood frozen as Lee sat on the floor thinking. Michael heard the sound of a waterfall. He turned and walked toward it, seeing a swimming pool that had a waterfall built inside. Its beauty struck him. "Michael," he heard whispered. He searched around to see where the whispering was coming from.

"I'm here. Turn and look in the pool; I'm inside the water."

A red scorpion fish danced before it put its head out of the water and stared at him. "It's me!"

Michael thought his eyes were playing a game with him when he saw the fish speaking to him. He closed his eyes, shook his head vigorously, and then opened his eyes again. The fish grew a little bigger and addressed him again by his name. "Michael, it's me—Frank! I'm the fish in front of you."

"Frank! I'm happy you found me. You look great."

"Have you lost your mind? What are you doing talking to a fish?" Lee said to Michael from behind.

"Frank is a spirit who protects me. Professor Wandom of the Spiritual Association of Livingstone assigned him to me. Professor Wandom is a close friend of my family."

"It was difficult to locate you. It was a long journey. How did you get here?" the fish asked.

Michael explained what had happened.

"Professor Wandom gave me this message to relate to you: 'you have a big show today, which you must win.' This woman you're dealing with, Azamerie, is a very powerful person. She's the queen of the ocean and controls everything that lives and breathes under the ocean. No creature or force has the power to stop her. So I have to help you to protect your father's secret code. You have a group of enemies trying to squeeze it out of you by any means possible. If you prevail after the show, you must ask her to send you back to Livingstone at once."

"Is she the only person who can get us out of here?"

"Yes. She has fabricated most of her citizens from various sea animals, but that isn't important now. All you have to do is take control of your confidence. The girls you're about to compete against are great magicians. They may also use their latest technologies to defeat you, but don't be worried, just do your best. I'll be there to help you when you need me. Take care of yourself, and I'll see you again." The fish disappeared.

When Michael turned, he almost ran into Lee, who was standing right behind him.

"So you were eavesdropping?" Michael asked.

"When I came close enough to eavesdrop, I couldn't hear a sound. What were you discussing with that fish?"

"Are you sure you didn't hear anything?"

"Not a sound. I'm serious!"

"Well, then, it's good you didn't."

"Why?"

"Long story."

They strolled to a little flower garden behind the pool.

"We have a big task ahead of us, and right now I don't know if my magic powers will even work here." Lee frowned as he sat at a nearby bench. "We're about to go out there. Azamerie respects you so much, and I hope that respect proliferates. Who knows how long this royal treatment will last?"

"We'll be fine; you don't have to panic. I've got us covered. Relax!" Michael said. "Get up; let's stroll around a little." Green, blue, and purple flowers manicured into the shapes of fish adorned the garden.

Lee suddenly felt like he was walking through mud. When he glanced down, he noticed that the ground was concrete. But as he moved, he felt as though his feet were damp and slopping through mud. He quickly called out for Michael. "Help! I'm stuck in mud."

When Michael saw him sinking, he ran over and pulled him up. His feet weren't soaked, and everything looked normal. Michael walked through the area several times, just to check.

"You think I was kidding? It was real. I can't believe it didn't happen to you! Why are all the bad things happening to me? I wish it would happen to you so you would believe me," Lee said angrily.

At that moment, Michael's entire body slipped under the concrete, leaving only his head out. He screamed for Lee. Lee ran and tried to hoist him by the head but couldn't. He took an iron hook from one of the gardens and started to dig, but the concrete around Michael's body sounded like iron clashing together.

"Michael, are you okay? I'll get you out soon." Michael's head suddenly slipped under the soil, and the area immediately became solid concrete, as if nothing had taken place.

Lee ran around searching for somebody to help, but he soon saw a huge concrete wall rapidly constructing itself around him. As he attempted to pass through, it promptly closed, leaving him ensnared. He cried out hoarsely, "Help!" His voice seemed stuck. He stopped calling and ran around the circular wall that trapped him, desperately trying to get out.

Michael fell between two tall, slim girls about his age. They were cleanly dressed in dark gray suits and black high-heeled boots that covered their knees. They looked at Michael with watery, dark brown eyes that peered out from a white complexion. They pouted their red lips and then began laughing at him. Michael had never seen so many beautiful women in one place before.

He swiftly stood up and said confidently, "Haven't you seen a man sink before?" He walked away from them as they kept eyeing him.

"What are you staring at?" he asked exasperatedly.

"We're just amazed because you appear languorously fragile. We were told that you are a great magician, but the way we got you down here was so effortless. I think we are going to start celebrating our victory," one of the women told him as they kept on laughing.

"Actually, the two of you are pretty, and frankly, I don't mind being here," Michael said smiling. "One thing I want you two to understand is you shouldn't judge me yet. Don't let this incident trick you into thinking my powers are weak. Where is this place, by the way?"

"You're beneath the earth. This is just a little room we constructed using our magic power. We forcibly brought you here so we could study whom we're competing against. We thought you were a great magician. By the way, your friend is in jail. Take a look."

They stood firmly in one position pointing their hands to the ground, and half of it suddenly changed into a television screen. They watched Lee pacing around confused.

"Are you guys really magicians?" one of the women asked.

"Why do you ask?"

"Because if you were the great magicians we heard about, it would've been easy for your friend to free himself by simply walking through those walls."

"Well, as great magicians, we were trained never to perform our magic uselessly, to prevent people from getting hurt." Michael hoped that he sounded strong and confident as Frank had urged him to be. It wasn't easy to watch these beautiful women and remain strong. "Why do you think they call us magicians? You think the title came easy?" He pushed himself toward them with confidence and said, "It is a pleasure meeting you."

Believing what Frank had told him earlier, Michael pointed his right hand above his head bravely and aluminum-ladder stairs roll down. He sauntered up the stairs, blowing a whistle with his hands in his pockets. The girls glanced at him, grinned, and then disappeared.

As he went up the steps, Michael saw Lee sitting with his head down. He gently touched his shoulder and asked what was wrong with him. Lee looked up and suddenly noticed that the wall has vanished. He became furious. "Stop playing with me!"

"Oh, now you think it's me?! You should know I would never do this to you."

"I saw you speaking to that fish earlier. You slipped under the ground pretending you were trapped, and you disappeared. Then I ended up trapped between walls, and now everything has vanished. What do you want me to believe? Please be nice and stop practicing your evil magic on me, or else I'll do something to you which you will never forget!" Lee angrily threatened.

"Wait a minute—you know I wouldn't do that to you," Michael said.

"You have been doing some strange things lately."

While they were talking, Azameraly appeared and said she had come to take them to the competition. Lee asked how many people were there.

"The entire city," she replied.

"Come on, let's go, and stop asking questions," Michael said, attempting to act confident.

They walked past her, but she asked them to stop. She grabbed their hands and suddenly they found themselves in the midst of the exhilarated crowd. Blue stage lights blared on the open-air stage. Michael tried to remember how Mioexfo had kept the crowd mesmerized. What did he do to keep the crowd enthralled? He wanted to finish the competition and get back to Livingstone. Azameraly showed them the way to the center of the stage before sneaking off to report to Azamerie.

The stadium was crammed, and women were cheerfully trying to touch Michael and Lee as they struggled from the back of the stage to the front.

"Get me out of here," Lee whispered.

"Don't panic! Just look confident," Michael replied.

Their competitors were already seated with their shoulders tall as if they were already victorious. They walked up to introduce themselves.

"Michael, Lee, we are Azashema and Joan.

It was a game for them *Funny names*, thought Michael. *Maybe their given name was Azas and their surname followed.* He'd make an effort to remember. He smiled broadly at the girls and then to Lee.

"This is the time to concentrate. Those girls are prepared. We have to appear confident, too." They sat down and waited for the announcer.

A tall, thin woman with a short bob told the crowd she was Azacromwe and began to introduce the contestants.

"Azashema and her sister, Joan, have travelled all the way from their hometown, Sipucher, to be with us tonight. They are the most powerful magicians the underworld has ever seen. Let's give them a round of applause." The crowd roared.

She introduced Michael and Lee as unknown magicians from Pluto. The crowd booed.

"Now look what you got me into," Lee whispered.

"Calm down!" Michael replied, keeping his shoulders high like the girls. "Raise your shoulders." Lee promptly arched his back, raising his shoulders.

Azacromwe explained that three judges would monitor the competition. They would provide instructions, and the contestants would be marked according to their accuracy and speed.

She then introduced the lead judge, Azachapladoe. The chubby woman walked on stage with a white scarf over her hair and said, "The rules are: one, no shaking hands; two, no talking to each other during the competition; three, stay in your seats until you're called upon; and four, no sticks, books, pens, or other magical items allowed. Only plain T-shirts and pants are to be worn; nothing else. You will be thoroughly searched before the competition. A contestant who disobeys the rules will be disqualified and dismissed immediately."

Azachapladoe asked each of them if they understood her. They nodded. Then she asked if they had any questions. They said no.

The crowd was cheering. The stadium was hot. The judge lifted up her arm to start the show, and the audience quieted down.

Azachapladoe began by asking the contestants to surprise the crowd. She pointed to Azashema and Joan. They walked to the middle of the stage and glanced at the crowd. They surprised the crowd by providing colored T-shirts, which fell from the sky like rain. Azachapladoe politely ordered them to stop when everyone had too many. The crowd cheered loudly.

A tough act to follow, thought Michael. Then the judges called their names. Michael and Lee stood in the middle of the stage glancing at each other. *How will we win over the audience?* Michael thought. He started to chant fake magical words, and Lee followed. Nothing happened. Where was Frank? Michael looked up at the ceiling then to both sides of the stage but couldn't find him. The crowd became noisy and wondered what was going on.

Azachapladoe called to them from the judge's station, "You must hurry, because we don't have much time." Michael begged for two more minutes, but Azachapladoe gave one, nothing more and nothing less.

They walked back to the center of the stage and the crowd, tired of waiting for them, began booing at them. Azashema and Joan smiled as Azamerie placed her palms over her face in embarrassment.

The judges were about to call for time out and mark that round against them, when the sky suddenly filled with white pigeons flying down carrying white roses in their beaks. The birds descended and spread among the crowd, sitting on the shoulders of people in the audience, including the judges and Azashema and Joan. The women took the roses from the birds' beaks and watched them fly away and disappear into the picturesque cloudy sky.

The rapturous view had many of the women in the audience crying with happiness. The judges were pleased, as were Michael and Lee.

Thanks, Frank, thought Michael, *wherever you are.*

It was a tight competition, and as the crowd clapped for them, Azashema and her sister stared at each other in dismay. They didn't expect the boys to be good magicians. The spectators and the judges appeared confused; they weren't sure who the winner would be now.

During the next round, the judges brought twenty-five gallons of fresh water in two big shoddy wooden barrels with two wooden straws. They asked the contestants to gulp it all within a period of a minute. In this round, they would work individually rather than as a team.

Azachapladoe called on Lee to start.

"How am I going to do this? I have no idea how to drink twenty-five gallons of water in one shot!" he blushed, and his eyes suddenly got red and watery as if he was about to cry.

"All you have to do is walk up there and drink it. Simple as that!" Michael said casually. Lee glared at him hard as fear flooded his veins, which began to protrude.

The judges kept calling his name, so Michael pushed him, and he entered the spotlight. The crowd was staring at him as he meandered with his shaking legs behind the barrel. He stared at the tank of water.

"You can do it. Just drink it." Lee heard the voice whispering from inside the barrel, and he saw a blue Siamese fighting fish staring at him, curiously swinging its tails.

"Are you talking to me?" Lee whispered back apprehensively.

"Yes, it's me, remember? You're Michael's friend, and I'm here to help you, so don't panic. My name is Frank. Enjoy the water and have fun," the fish spoke and disappeared.

"We're running out of time here! We give you thirty seconds to drink that water. If you don't, we'll disqualify you from this round!" Azachapladoe warned.

Michael screamed, telling him to do it, as Azashema and Joan sat back grinning. Lee gulped the entire tank within thirty seconds, and then sauntered away belching and licking his mouth. He stared at Azashema and her sister.

The judges carefully examined the barrel and the area around it and concluded that he had followed all the rules.

"You did it!" Michael embraced him tightly. Lee told him about Frank. Michael was shocked but remained calm with a crafty smile. "Now we are safe. I want you to keep your head held high."

Lee arched his back, raising his shoulders again with his eyes wild and watchful.

The judges called on Joan. She went up, drank the water rapidly, and walked back to her seat as if it were natural.

During the third and final round, they brought in a Vxantrick, a hideous and fearsome two-headed leopard in a big silver box, placed it in the middle of the stadium, and then let it out. Its rancid odor filled the entire arena. The black leopard was large enough to eat Michael and still thirst for Lee. Its long, round tail was equipped with a sharp, razor-like edge. It had red eyes, four mighty legs, and thick, long, sharp claws, and it weighed over a thousand pounds. Its teeth were sharp as knives and frightened the crowd.

Azachapladoe quickly assured the audience that they were safe as she pleaded for their patience.

"Ladies, although this is the most dangerous and poisonous leopard in the entire world, you are safe. Our talented magicians can handle the Vxantric. Contestants, this is the last round. Your instructions are to calm the Vxantric, but first, stand still and let it bite you as many times as it can, showing the audience how his bites cannot affect you. After, when you let it try to eat you, calm it down and show the audience how the Vxantric can become a pussy cat."

Some people in the crowd vomited from the stench the Vxantric was spraying from its body. Michael and Lee began to tremble, as they were both afraid of leopards. Michael thought he heard Frank say, "Be confident." He held his legs firm and held his head high.

The judges called on Azashema and Joan to face the Vxantric. Michael breathed a sigh of relief. Their eyes were wide with fear, but they pretended to look normal. As they approached the Vxantric, it grew angrier and rapidly dashed at them. It started biting them instantaneously, injecting as much poison into their bodies from its putrid mouth as it could manage. The bites penetrated their bodies, and the poison spread. The girls crumpled on the floor and moaned loudly.

The judges rushed onto the stage trying to scare the Vxantric off. But by that point, it grew more aggressive and tried to viciously tear anyone who approached the girls it was attempting to eat.

Michael's face blanched. "Let's get out of here." Lee grew dreadfully afraid, and the boys decided to withdraw from that round.

The girls were struggling for their lives as white saliva foam blasted from their mouths. With the anger the Vxantric had generated, thick, red fire flew from its mouth and almost burned the judges as they ran around trying to help the girls.

Michael was looking in every direction because he heard his name. There was a little black butterfly with yellowish wings sitting on his right shoulder.

"I'm right here," Frank said. Michael carefully took the butterfly and held it in his right palm. "You boys should stop shaking and go over there to save those girls quickly. They will die if you don't. Don't worry; I'll do all the work for you. Just stand there and pretend. If the Vxantric strikes you, don't worry; I will restore you as if nothing happened."

"Are you Frank?" Michael softly asked.

The butterfly didn't reply and disappeared.

A Brutal Attack

"It isn't about the contest anymore; it's about saving them!" Michael said as he moved hastily forward, and Lee promptly followed.

They quickly went nearer to the Vxantric and warned the judges to vacate the area immediately. But the judges were still trying to fight the Vxantric, so Michael had to scream at them. They backed away a little and stood nearby, anxiously prepared to help.

The mad Vxantric started viciously striking them with thick fire, but Michael and Lee kept approaching. The Vxantric kicked them hard. They flew onto the judges and fell then, undeterred, swiftly got up and ran back. But this time, the Vxantric tightly wrapped its huge muscular legs around them both. Its odor nauseated them.

The Vxantric bit Lee on the head, making a sound like two very sharp irons grinding together. It was so loud that the spectators covered their ears. The Vxantric also tried biting Michael, but his neck turned into iron. At that moment, a little human head with a small, round mouth and a big, flat nose emerged from Michael's left shoulder, glared at the Vxantric, and seemed to talk to it. The human head was Frank.

"Who are those boys?" the ferocious leopard spoke in a deep, aggressive voice.

"Magicians," the human head answered.

"They are very powerful. I'll let them go, but leave the girls to me so I can feast on them!"

"Can't do that. The boys want them saved or they'll finish you. You don't want to die. Let them go and your life will be spared," said the human head as he bounced around Michael's shoulder.

"I'll let you save those girls, but bring me food later because I am ravenously hungry!" the Vxantric said.

"You have a deal," the human head said and disappeared. The Vxantric backed away from Michael and Lee, who rushed to the girls and dragged them to the judges' station.

"Please, don't let anyone touch them because they are covered with a deadly poison from the Vxantric," Michael warned. But one of the judges recklessly took Azashema by the hand in an effort to revive her. Right then, the poison flew through her body and consumed her entire skin, leaving her skeleton scattered. The other judges screamed as they ran fearfully away.

Michael got a bucket of water with Lee's help. They washed the poison and the slime off the girls' bodies. Michael asked Lee to point his fingers toward the girls quickly. He did so as the spectators that had not left the stadium watched, gasping.

White rays of lights suddenly flew out of his fingers and entered the girls' noses. Ten seconds later, they vomited thick blood, and then stood up and fearfully glanced around, trying to escape the vicinity. Michael moved to hold them and gently told them to relax and that everything was all right.

The remaining crowd was on fire. Michael and Lee quickly asked the judges to supply some raw meat to the Vxantric before it killed the entire city. The judges ran to ask Azamerie for meat.

She pointed her fingers to the middle of the field, and suddenly, a fat cow appeared. The Vxantric began consuming it.

When it was full, it suddenly vanished, leaving no trace.

"Where did you get that Vxantric?" Michael asked the judges curiously.

"I saw it lying by the roadside one morning on my way to work," said Azachapladoe who turned to look at Michael. "I stopped to stare at it. It looked so beautiful I fell in love with it. It wasn't that big, and it was fun to be around. I've had it for five days now. I felt it was perfect for this competition; that's why I brought it here. But as soon as it got here, it started growing bigger."

"You're very lucky it didn't eat you," Michael said.

"You're right; I'm scared to go home because it might have gone there."

At that moment, Azamerie furiously walked off, and the judges cancelled the competition without a tally.

Azashema and her sister Joan walked up to Michael and Lee.

"Thank you for saving our lives. We are leaving, but we promise to see you tomorrow since we now know where to find you." Joan winked at them.

"Wait!" Michael said, "How old are you girls?"

"We're twelfths," Azashema answered. "We're fraternal twins. And you?"

"I am twelve; he is thirteen," Michael answered.

Everybody had abandoned them at the stadium. Michael and Lee stood there waiting for someone to take them home. It was getting dark, and still no one showed up.

"I think we should stay here for the night. We can find our way back in the morning. That malicious woman just used us and dumped us," Michael said.

"You know what I am thinking?" Lee asked.

"No, what?"

"How we can get back to Livingstone. I think the longer we stay in Texdulonicram, the worse things will become."

* * * * *

"What were you thinking, Professor Barclay? Did you want to destroy all of us with that beast?" Azamerie said, looking into the screen in her home.

"Take it easy, Azamerie. I didn't know it would grow so big. When I sent it to Texdulonicram, it was no more than a few feet tall."

"I told you, I only wanted the girls destroyed, not the whole town."

"Find out the code, Azamerie."

"You're not giving me enough time."

"Fine, I'll give you another week. Otherwise, I will bring them back and our deal is off. Leo will find out the code for me. Right, Leo?"

Leo stood alongside Professor Barclay, nodding his head as his eyes twitched with fear.

"One more week," said Azamerie as she turned off the screen with the remote.

* * * * *

Later that night, Azamerie suddenly appeared before the boys and respectfully apologized. "My mistresses actually forgot about you."

"We'll accept your apology for today and hope it won't be repeated," Lee warned.

Without answering, she swiftly took them to an unknown location. It was a big house surrounded by sharp iron fans. As soon they began studying the area, she vanished.

"She's entrapped us!" Lee exclaimed.

At that moment, they found themselves standing on a tiny island surrounded by boiling water emitting copious amounts of steam as if they were in a sauna.

"Where is this place?" Michael asked anxiously.

"I don't know. I think she brought us here to kill us!" They stood there numbly, prepared for the worst.

All of a sudden, thousands of agitated white rats sped toward them. They had no place to run—only through the boiling water. They pinpointed a waiting position and stood prepared.

"Where are they coming from?" Lee asked Michael.

"I think they're coming from under the island. They look very aggressive and ravenous! At the slightest mistake we make, they will overpower us!"

To their surprise, the rats started appearing from all directions, gathered in long lines, and in no time, they were on top of them. Michael and Lee wrestled hard, throwing the rats into the water, but they kept coming. Rats were flying everywhere in a white flurry. As the rats dropped in the water, they were burned and boiled.

"They're biting me," Lee screamed.

"Me, too," Michael said.

"Can't you use your prince stuff to get us out of here?" Lee fought hard, pushing one away and then another. "Where's your friend, Frank?"

"Don't know." They had managed to throw all the rats into the water when they saw bigger rats approach in one long line. They fought hard for almost an hour and a half before killing them all. They were breathing heavily, waiting to see what would come next.

Suddenly, Michael and Lee saw a bright light flashing and approaching from afar.

Lee turned and told Michael, "I think it's your friend. He's coming to save us."

"We can't be sure. He has never come like that before. He always surprises me, but I think he's a good man."

"Man?" said Lee, "I never considered him that way." Without talking, they decided to pay close attention to the light. Earlier, Lee had told Michael that light could be distracting them from a deadly attack. Oddly, as it got closer, it appeared smaller and smaller, until it touched the island.

"I don't care what happens; we must stick together." Lee moved toward Michael and held his right hand tight, staring at the little strange light.

Then they heard a familiar voice, and Lee said, "I know that voice."

"Who is that?" Michael asked in a squeaky voice.

"I think it is Azamerie, that despicable sorcerer."

As they watched closely and carefully, they saw a petite honeybee emerging from the light and flying around them in a full circle. It came and stood in front of them and immediately transmogrified into Azamerie.

She was dressed in white and had a big round hat and a white cane in her right hand. She wore white gloves on her hands. She was laughing madly as she strolled around them. She glanced at them in disgust as if they were shoddy, but Michael and Lee carefully watched her every move and prepared for the worst.

"I now have you in my killing ground. Here, I can do anything I want with you. But first, I want to welcome you to my little woman-made island. I name it Bodeth. Do you know what I do to people who enter here? I feed on them. Do you know why I am desperate to kill you?" she asked politely with a grin.

They stayed quiet, watching her next move closely.

"It's because you have allowed Azashema and her evil little sister Joan to survive. I wanted them dead, and it was the perfect time, and you two screwed it up! Now you must pay. I will bite you until you feel my teeth crashing through your bones, and after, I will eat you alive!" she grinned hard.

"If you think you'll kill us, you'd better think again. We might end up killing you first!" Michael said boldly.

"The only way you can save yourselves is if the prince here reveals his father's code. Otherwise, I think I've had enough of your nonsense! This is the time to do what you won't believe I'm capable of doing to evil little creatures like you!"

"I don't know the code," Michael said, remembering Frank's warning.

"I don't believe you, fool. Think you can trick the great Azamerie?" she roared.

"How blind are you? After all you've seen, you still have the audacity to come after us. You should be afraid of our shadows!" Lee said bravely.

At this, she became angrier and immediately transformed into a five-foot-tall gorilla with two big, long front teeth that resembled nails.

The gorilla didn't scare Michael and Lee because they thought Frank was still with them. It jumped around them many times grunting aloud, but it didn't attack. It stood in front of them, and then transformed back to Azamerie.

"That didn't scare you?" she asked.

"Not at all," Michael said, shifting calmly from one leg to another.

"You are prepared for this, aren't you?" she mocked. "I, the great Azamerie, have the power to transmogrify into anything I choose." Her body began to transform into a Vxantric identical to the one they had fought against at the competition.

The boys didn't know that Azamerie actually did not want to kill them. She wanted the boys as slaves and to scare them into sharing the secret code with her.

Michael and Lee laughed with confidence. The Vxantric grew larger until it was the same size as the beast at the competition. They still weren't scared, however, they didn't know that Frank had left them and travelled back to Livingstone thinking they were safe. To their surprise, the Vxantric begin to walk toward them little by little. As the Vxantric took a step, the island vibrated.

"This is the same kind of Vxantric that almost eliminated Joan and her sister," Lee said, frightened. "Just tell her the code and get us out of here," he whispered to Michael.

"I don't know it," Michael whispered back. He was becoming nervous but didn't want to show it. He remained quiet and started panicking about what Azamerie would do next. He thought about what Frank had told him earlier: that he should relax and fight his battles with confidence.

"I will kill you and let the rats feast on your flesh, and you will be exterminated from the face of your world forever!" Michael said furiously as they prepared themselves for battle.

The Vxantric accelerated toward them as brown dust flew beneath it. It snarled at Michael and Lee and began shooting fire from its left mouth. The fire was so strong that it burnt off pieces of their shirts.

Michael and Lee became nervous and moved a little farther back. They stretched their hands and pointed their fingers toward the Vxantric. It stopped and watched as it licked its mouths. The boys chanted and nothing happened. They repeated their motions for about a minute and still withheld their powers. The Vxantric began to wonder what they were doing. When they realized nothing was happening, they glanced at each other in great trepidation.

"Just make up a code," Lee whispered in Michael's ear.

The Vxantric ran and struck them with its body; they flew and fell close to the water. The boys got up and saw the Vxantric speeding at them. They quickly ran away from the water.

"We should separate," Lee suggested.

"Where do you want to go? Can't you see we are surrounded by this hot water? I say we stay close together," Michael suggested as he began to shiver.

The Vxantric laid down flat and positioned both of its heads toward them. It started attacking them with thick fire, which flew from its mouths like red tennis balls and struck like bombs. They dodged the fire as they ran around it. The Vxantric was attacking them from every angle. The fire burnt off some of the hair on their heads. They were black from the smoke and had nowhere to escape to.

"Just make up a code," Lee repeated. "Call Azamerie and tell her you will give her the code."

The Vxantric pushed closer and began thumping its huge long legs on them until they could barely move. Then it wrapped its legs around Michael and Lee and licked their faces with its sandpaper tongue. They saw themselves close to the Vxantric's mouths and saw thick, reddish slime coming out of the mouths.

The boys screamed loudly as the Vxantric slashed their shoulders with its teeth and began licking their blood as it flowed. They tried to fight back, but the Vxantric held them tightly and they couldn't move their bodies.

"I'm only thirteen, too young to die!" Lee pleaded.

At this, the Vxantric paused and positioned its body firmly on the ground. The head on the left rolled up close to them. It pulled back a little and opened its mouth wide as though it was about to devour them. They screamed with all their might, and suddenly the Vxantric's body changed into Azamerie's.

"We meet again! Now give me the secret code of your father's powers, and I will set you free." She spoke in a thunderous voice.

"Oh, it's you. I do not know what you are talking about," Michael pleaded.

"Give her a fake one," whispered Lee, touching his friend's battered shoulder.

"I heard that," Azamerie lifted her large hat. "Think you can trick the great Azamerie! Well, you can't. No one can." She laughed. "You could've killed me when you had the opportunity. You boys were pretty strong at the competition. Where are your powers now? The Vxantric likes eating young boys like you, so today will be the day I will feast and celebrate. It will eat you alive slowly, very slowly." She gestured with her hands to demonstrate. "I don't care what you say to me. I won't let you get away from me!"

"Listen! I have diamonds in my pocket. I'll give them all to you if you let us go," Lee begged, crying.

"The Vxantric can't eat diamonds, but it can eat you!" Azamerie's eyes glowered over them. "Michael, give me the code and live."

"I don't know what you are talking about," Michael said.

"Well, I will miss you boys. Have a nice time in the Vxantric's belly." Azamerie transmogrified again into the beast.

"You got me into this," Lee cried to Michael, "now get me out."

The Vxantric lifted the boys, moved its head, and began to squeeze them hard and tight as they struggled to breathe. It used its sharp teeth to slash their skin slowly as it licked their blood greedily. They cried out painfully for help, calling all the names they knew.

Vxantric Trouble

Michael and Lee began to lose blood. They were getting weaker and weaker and knew that their chances of surviving were slim.

"Put the boys down, you ugly stinking Vxantric!" a sharp female voice cried out.

The Vxantric turned around speedily and suddenly saw Joan and Azashema. It ignored their demand and continued to lick the boys' blood.

The boys were unable to see the girls from their position, but they could hear their voices.

"Please save us!" Michael screamed out as the Vxantric's tongue continued to scratch their skins.

Joan and her sister madly struck the Vxantric on its front legs. The Vxantric saw them and roughly kicked them with its back leg. They flew and fell close to the water. The Vxantric still kept the boys in its clutches. The girls quickly arose and ran closer, but the Vxantric used its left head to attack them with fire. The girls were doing everything they could to get the beast to drop the boys, but it wouldn't. They fought for almost an hour before the Vxantric weakened and released Michael and Lee.

"Run quickly!" Azashema shrieked at them. The boys were exhausted but managed to limp away as the girls kept the Vxantric occupied.

The beast moved speedily toward the girls, but they were solidly prepared this time. Without moving, they watched it carefully as it approached, eager to destroy them. Together they stretched their hands and threw a long white piece of cloth, which the Vxantric sniffed into its right nostril. A heavy scent of rotten eggs spread from the cloth.

The beast stopped and tried to blow the smell out, but it wouldn't come out. The Vxantric grew angrier and started attacking them with firebombs from both mouths, striving to kill them faster. The girls were leaping in all directions in order to avoid being hit as they kept the beast's attention off the boys. But soon it grew wise to their plans and turned back to Michael and Lee, shooting firebombs in their direction.

The girls quickly moved the boys from the line of fire, laying them at the far edge of the island. The Vxantric grew bigger and taller again—over seven feet.

"Wait here. We will be back for you," Azashema said, and Michael smiled weakly at her.

The girls wanted to confuse the Vxantric, but failed to realize that since it had two heads it could see full circle. At that point, it pretended to be hurt, and the girls came closer to finish it off, when it suddenly hit Joan. She flew up in the air and collapsed on the rough earth, letting out a loud yelp. Azashema was still fighting the Vxantric as brown dust flew upwards.

"I know what we can use to exterminate this animal!" Joan told Michael.

"What?" Michael asked anxiously.

"I think our magic powers can't wobble it. It keeps getting bigger and stronger the more we try to hurt it. If I had yellow diamonds, I could use them to increase our powers and wipe this beast out."

"I have lots of diamonds, which I took without permission from my father's jewelry store to show my friends at Thorn Valley but the situation changed," Lee told her. He took them out and offered them to her. Holding her side, she painfully stood up and screamed at her sister to continue keeping the Vxantric at bay.

As soon as Azashema turned to listen to her sister, the Vxantric kicked her hard with its front right leg like a football, almost tearing her flesh from her legs. She flew and landed at the boys' feet, nearly in tears from the force of the blow. The Vxantric sped aggressively toward them. Joan told Lee to point the largest diamond toward the Vxantric.

Joan stretched out her right hand toward the diamond; a brilliant light shot from it like lightning and entered the diamond. She told Lee to throw the diamond toward the Vxantric when it came closer.

The sisters quickly pulled back from Lee, who rotated toward them and asked, "What are you doing?"

"Don't be scared! If you do as I tell you, we will all be fine. Now look, it's getting closer!" Joan cried.

Lee threw the diamond at the Vxantric, and it blasted like thunder. The sound was so explosive that it shook the land and threw them all closer to the boiling water.

They saw a bright light sparkling and shooting into the sky like a firecracker. The heat was unbearable, and they couldn't see anything due to the shiny lights, which began melting the Vxantric's skin off as it cried in pain. The Vxantric burned to the ground, its brown bones smoldering with hot, black smoke.

Michael quickly ran to Azashema, lifted her up, and thanked her.

"Well, I think we are even now. We saved each other's lives."

"Come, let's make sure this Vxantric is dead for good," Michael told them.

They carefully approached the mound of bones. Slimy blood flowed out of one of the skull bones and penetrated the ground.

"We must do something fast, otherwise, in a couple of hours, it could regenerate!" Joan said. "What shall we do now?"

"You still have more diamonds?" Azashema asked.

Lee gave her the bag of diamonds. She took one and gave it to her sister, asking her to hold it close to the bones at the exact location where the blood was flowing from.

As Azashema did so, Joan performed the same routine they had done earlier and asked her sister to cover the diamonds with the hot skull bones. They rose and moved back. Joan stretched her fingers toward the diamond, but no light shot out this time. After a couple of seconds, the diamond suddenly exploded like a grenade, burning and crushing the remaining bones completely. A sharp noise pierced their eardrums, and they all instinctively shielded their ears tightly using their palms. The noise went on for several minutes.

The boys and girls carefully began to investigate the area but found nothing. They celebrated by embracing each other. At least for now, they were safe. Lee said he could heal everyone's wounds. He asked them to sit in a semi-circle on the earthen ground. Lee sat in front of them, closed his eyes, and meditated for a few seconds. He opened his eyes, walked up to Joan, and squeezed her wounds with his right hand. She screamed from the pain that ran through her entire body. Then Lee slapped his palm on the ground and walked over to her sister. He gently rubbed his right palm on her wound. He ambled to Michael and covered his wounds with his palm. He asked them to stand up, and they did so easily. They looked down and saw they were healed.

Joan told Lee to heal himself, because he still had bleeding wounds all over his body. "My magic doesn't work on me—only on others."

"I didn't know you could do that," Michael said. "I also didn't know you had a pile of diamonds in your pocket. Why didn't you give one to the cashier in the restaurant so we wouldn't have had to shine those floors?"

"I wanted to return them to my father, that's why."

"Why?"

"Because his jewelry store doesn't make a lot of money. I only brought them to show my friends, because last summer my friends at Thorn Valley said that if my father really owned a diamond store, they wanted to see proof."

"Who's going to heal you, Lee?" Joan asked.

"I'll make sure he's all right as soon we get to the city," Michael promised.

"Well, we have to hurry and get out of here before something changes," Azashema said.

They walked toward the boiling water. "The only way out of this place is through this water," Lee said.

"It will take us four hours to get to the city from here," Joan said.

"We don't care how long it takes. All we want is to get out of this place," Lee said.

"We can fly with you, but we will have to pass across the ocean. The other alternative is to hold hands and disappear. It will still take four hours, but we won't notice," Azashema said.

"I think we should disappear together," Michael said. They all held hands and the girls chanted and prayed to their magic gods. Soon they disappeared.

* * * * *

They found themselves standing at the stadium. The city was normal, and everyone was going about their usual business.

"Let's go to Azamerie's palace and see what's going on there," Michael suggested.

They took a transit bus. When they entered the palace, the scene shocked them. The palace was destroyed inside as if a war had been fought. Scars of black smoke marred its decorative walls. Pieces of white furniture lay scattered about the dining area. The multitier chandelier was torn from the ceiling. Large fish lay dead everywhere.

"I think Azamerie selfishly killed them all before going to see you guys on the island," Joan said.

"Why?" Michael asked.

"Who knows? Everything that woman did was strange. Let's go inform the city about what happened."

They went out into the public square, but this time the crowd gloated over them.

"It's the magicians. Hurry, let's go look," Michael could hear them say. Quickly he got the crowd's attention and then broke the news about their queen's death.

One of the elderly women curiously asked from far behind, "Are you sure she's really dead? We know who she is." Michael explained everything. The crowd cheered, and some embraced with joy while others clicked their cameras after calling out Michael's name.

"Hold on!" Michael said. The crowd quieted.

"Azamerie's death could cause this city to drown within a couple of years. We'll stay here for two more days until you find a legitimate leader. We'll also make sure everything is in order before we leave," Michael said and dismissed them.

A woman squeezed her way to the front and voluntarily offered to shelter them for the time they were there. Marizama, a tall and chubby woman over fifty with fluffy brown hair, looked at them with far-away blue eyes.

"There are so many of us. Where will you stay?" Michael laughed.

"Don't worry about me. I will sleep in my living room if I have to."

"Are you girls coming with us?" Michael turned to look at the sisters.

"Yes, but we won't sleep in the same room," Joan clarified.

"That's fine with us," Lee said.

They followed her without asking for her name; they were too exhausted and just wanted a bath and some sleep. The group walked for a few minutes, and the woman led them to one of the large houses lined in a row in a neighborhood of original, sprawling homes. She strolled ahead to open the door and welcomed them in. The door slammed heavily when she closed it.

"You have a nice place here," Azashema complimented her.

"Thank you. I actually got most of my furniture from my bountiful friends. Come, let me show you where you'll be sleeping." After she showed both pairs their rooms, they told her that they hadn't seen a house so richly decorated before. The front room's ceiling almost reached the roof, and their voices echoed when they spoke.

"This is so classy," said Joan.

Michael and Lee's room was attractively decorated with rich green wallpaper. The two custom-made, mahogany, queen-sized beds still left enough space in the room to run around.

"Nice," Lee said, feeling the surface of one of the beds.

"How are your wounds?" Michael asked.

"They're still the same, but they will heal in a couple of days."

"We should ask for some hot water to clean them and kill the bacteria. Wait here, I'll get the water," Michael volunteered.

Michael opened the door; when he closed it and took a step forward, he suddenly stumbled across a hideous creature sitting erect and gazing at him. Its body was like a dark-brown mountain deer, with a female human head with two brown horns sitting on each side. As soon as the creature saw Michael, it transformed into their hostess.

"Do you want something?" she asked as Michael stood frozen.

"Actually, no, I'm fine. I don't want anything." He quickly went back into his room and his knees almost buckled. He told Lee what he had just seen and suggested they leave the house immediately. But Lee was exhausted.

"Leave her alone; she won't kill us." Lee said and fell on the bed. His tired eyelids pulled his eyes shut.

"I must go tell Azashema and her sister about this."

Lee opened his eyes again. "No. Leave the girls alone; let them rest. We had a rough day. Can't you see that the people in this city will think twice before attempting to attack us in any way? Didn't you see how they greeted us? When you saw that, you should have been brave. You're a magician now. Please, if you don't want to rest, that's fine, but I do, so talk to me when I wake up." Lee closed his eyes and put the feather-filled cover over his head.

"Okay."

Michael sat in the chair for a couple of minutes, but he wasn't satisfied. He went to find their host and saw her in the kitchen preparing some food. He tactfully greeted her, and she grinned at him innocently.

"What is your name?" Michael asked.

"Call me Marizama." He introduced himself as well. She stared at him and asked, "Are you all right?"

"Why do you ask?"

"I can see in your eyes that you want to ask me something."

"Yes, I sure do, but first finish what you're doing."

Marizama turned back to continue dicing onions and put them in her bowl of lettuce and tomatoes. Michael continued to stroll around the house. He turned the corner from the kitchen and saw a large hallway with colorful paintings hanging on the white walls. The home was decorated like an art gallery. He stood looking at the paintings and then envisioned the house from the outside. It wasn't large enough to contain such a huge, long hallway. He wondered if maybe he was in a huge basement. He decided to walk through the hallway. After a bit, Michael noticed that he had walked a long distance and couldn't clearly see where the starting point was. He decided to return to Marizama.

He found Marizama sitting in her office reading. She looked up and politely asked him to have a seat. Marizama dropped her book on the desk and stared methodically at him.

"Who are you?" Michael asked.

"I'm a woman you don't want to know about. I advise you not to ask me such questions again."

"I demand to know, and I want you to tell me the truth!"

"All right, I'll tell you." Michael looked at her skeptically. "I'm a ghost," she proudly exclaimed.

Michael moved back. "Are you sure?"

"Come closer. Give me your hands." She took his right hand and laid it on her left chest. He couldn't feel her heartbeat, and her body was cold. She took him to a big mirror in the hallway, and they stood in front of it close together, but only his image appeared.

"That's great magic!" Michael said. "How long have you been living in this city?"

"For 923 years and I'm still very young, but this is one of the best cities in the underworld. Nobody cares about who you are or how much riches you have. Everybody just tries to squeeze themselves into their corners. In fact, it's hard to make friends around here. The city is diverse with people from the four corners of the earth. Where did you learn your magic?" she asked.

"It's genetic. I was actually born with it, and it can even move mountains," Michael proudly boasted. He didn't mention that he often needed Frank's help.

"I know a lot about magic, but I'm not too good at it yet. Follow me; let me show you something." She got up and Michael followed. They walked deep into the hallway and came across a big, white wall with seven different doors of different colors. Marizama stood close to one of the doors and asked him, "Do you know what I have behind these doors?"

"No."

She opened the yellow door and asked him to come closer and look inside. The room was filled with sparkling blue water. He could see different kinds of fishes of various colors swimming in all directions as if they were in a mighty aquarium.

Michael moved very close and took a taste of the water. It was salty. He turned to Marizama, "Is this seawater?"

"Yes, it is." Marizama walked to the door. "Excuse me for a minute; I'll be right back."

Leaving Michael at the doors, she walked into a nearby office with a looming screen in one corner and a green sofa in the other. She sat on the chesterfield and clicked the button on the black remote control.

"Okay, Professor, they're here with me," she told the face in the screen. "I need money for arrears on my house. Can I get a deposit?"

Professor Barclay turned his swivel chair to face Marizama head-on. "No money for partial work. Try for the code first or finish him off. No in-betweens for payment. Got it?"

"Yes, sir," said Marizama.

"I hope you'll do a better job than Azamerie."

Attacked by a Snapper

Marizama walked back into the room she left Michael in, faced the wall, and washed her hands. Michael saw a beautiful red snapper and gently thrust his right hand inside the water to touch it, noticing that it was larger than he thought.

As soon as he turned to call Marizama, the snapper swiftly grabbed his hand and started dragging him into the water. Michael was wrestling to pull out his hand, but he could feel the strong current as the snapper pulled. He began to scream, calling Marizama for help. She glanced at him and laughed madly.

"I'm not pretending here! This fish wants to kill me! Please get me out of here!"

She stood back with her hands folded across her chest as she watched in silence, grinning.

Michael's face had entered the water. When he opened his eyes, he saw his hand in Marizama's mouth. She had entered the water and was holding the snapper's body, pulling him harder. Michael was forced into water. Within a couple of seconds, however, he realized he could breathe and talk normally.

After freeing his hand from Marizama's mouth, who was no longer in the water, he noticed that the fishes all around him had human heads. He began conversing with them.

One conversation led to another, and while discussing the beauty of the ocean, one of men boastfully exclaimed, "We are evil forces that persistently torment humans to become cruel to one another." They laughed proudly. Michael stared at them, wondering what he was doing conversing with such demonic people.

"Demons is the perfect name for guys like you. You are all demons." Michael laughed.

They became outraged and viciously attacked him. Some even tried to bite his ears off. They shoved him from one position to another until he fell out of the water. He stood up and noticed his body and his clothes were dry then he saw Marizama starting to close the door. He jumped up and ran out of the room.

"They're crazy!" Michael screeched. "What did you do in there?"

"It's actually one of my exit routes from this city. It takes me to the Kingdom of Xludosen; I have lots of friends living there."

"How do you go there? Do you swim?"

"Of course, but I usually walk because I have certain powers that work better under water."

"Do they have a city like this in Xludosen too?"

"Oh, yes. They have lots of cities much more beautiful than this, where you find both men and women with children. Those cities are everywhere, far into the underworld."

"This opens my eyes to see a lot of things my forefathers never had the opportunity to see," Michael said in contemplation.

"Let's go back before your friends start searching for us."

"Oh no, I want to see what's behind the other doors," Michael demanded. His experience had made him forget about finding hot water for Lee.

Disappointingly, he suddenly found himself with Marizama standing in the kitchen where he had first started. Michael walked out of the kitchen to see through the hallway again, but it had vanished. He went back in and stared hard at her. She started laughing.

"You behave like you're naïve. I think you still have lots to learn," she said.

"How do the women in Texdulonicram make babies without a man?" Michael asked Marizama.

She was struck by his question and asked, "How old are you?"

"I'm twelve. But I learned about the female reproductive system in school."

"Things are very different here. Women don't know about sex like they do in other kingdoms. Azamerie gave them both female and male reproductive organs." She smiled at him. "You ask a lot of questions."

"You are right. When you have a child, you will realize that they ask too many questions, because they're eager to expand their knowledge."

"You are right," she agreed.

"Can I help you around the kitchen?"

Marizama looked appreciatively at Michael. "Sure, here, take this broom and clean up the living room." Michael took the broom and began to sweep the dustless floor. After a few minutes, he gave Marizama the broom back.

"Thank you. Now you can take a rest."

"I'm not tired; I want to stay here to see how you do your cooking." He suddenly had an odd feeling that she might poison their food.

While they were talking, Joan and her sister came into the kitchen asking, "How are you guys doing?" Michael greeted them back.

After a while Azashema asked, "Where is Lee?"

"Oh, I forgot about him! I'll be right back." Michael ran to the room and saw Lee lying in bed completely covered with spider webs as if he had been lying there for ages. Michael managed to reach through the webs. He grabbed Lee's leg and shook it hard to wake him up, but he couldn't. Michael panicked and tried again more forcefully to pull both legs, but Lee still did not wake up. Now, he wasn't even breathing. "Lee, wake up! Don't leave me here alone. Wake up!"

Michael was frightened and yelled out to the girls, who came running. When they entered the room, they couldn't believe what they saw.

The three of them quickly tried to clean up the spider webs, but the longer ones were very hard and strong. They ran to kitchen for knives in order to cut the webs.

"Let's get him off the bed to see what is happening with him," said Azashema.

"No. Leave him right there," Marizama said standing at the doorway. "He isn't here at this moment. He travelled far away, but he'll be back shortly."

"How do you know that?" Michael asked fearfully. Other than the girls, Lee was his only friend in Texdulonicram. Michael hoped he would wake up soon. They still had to get back to Thorn Valley together.

"Whenever you see spider webs like this on top of a person while they are asleep, it means they have traveled someplace," Marizama replied.

"Okay, I'll stand here until he comes back," Michael said.

"If he returns and he sees anybody in this room, he'll go back to where he was and won't return. If you love your friend and want him to be with you soon, we should all leave this room now and wait in the living room," Marizama warned.

Joan asked Michael to do as Marizama said. They all walked out of the bedroom, and then she turned the light off and closed the door. They sat in the living room while Marizama set the table in the dining room and brought in the food. She then called them.

"We won't eat without Lee. I'm sorry," Michael said.

"Are you serious? Suppose he doesn't come back? Does that mean you won't eat at all?" she asked.

"Yes," they agreed in unison.

"But please don't say that," Michael added.

Marizama covered the food, and then sat with them. The room was quiet and everyone was worried as they carefully watch Lee's window from the living room.

After a couple of hours, they saw bright shining lights fill Lee's entire room.

"Lee's back," Marizama said. The light shone for a few more minutes and then went off.

"Can I go there now?" Michael asked Marizama.

"No. Wait and go there in one hour."

But before too long, Lee walked out of the room smiling. His face was shining with sparkles of white light. Michael ran and tried to hug him, however, he ran right through him and fell.

"Where were you?" Michael asked, lifting himself off the floor.

"You won't believe this!" Lee began, "I was with Professor Barclay and Professor Oden. They were happy to see me and were wondering how you were doing. I explained everything and told them that they will be seeing us shortly."

"Why is your face blinking with light?" Michael asked.

"Don't worry about it. Some of the light came back with me from my travel," Lee said and turned to his friend. "I missed you."

They tried to embrace each other again, but Michael's body slipped through him again, as if he were passing through the wind. He couldn't touch Lee at all. Fear flooded him.

"You go back in there and get into your body because this isn't you! You're not human right now."

"What do you mean?" Lee asked in alarm.

"Just go back in the bedroom and lie on top of your body on the bed. When you feel you have re-entered your body then you can come back here to us," Marizama clarified.

"What are you guys talking about? I'm still who I am even though you can't feel me. I haven't changed in any way. Why are you playing with me?"

"We are not joking with you. The fact is you are now a ghost. To prove this, you can come with me."

Lee followed Michael into the kitchen. Michael asked him to take a cup and give it to him.

"Why do you want me to do that?"

"To prove to you that you're not who you think you are."

Lee turned to take the cup, but his right hand slipped through it. He repeated this twice and was still not able to lift the cup.

"This is it!" He smiled widely. "I'm a real magician now! I can pass through anything, and nothing can hurt me ever again. That ugly Vxantric can't ever hurt me anymore!" he said happily.

"You go in there right now and do as I say; that's an order!" Michael said.

"Are you out of your mind? I don't need that body anymore. You guys can see me, right?"

"Sure we can see you," Joan answered.

"Then I'll stay like this to protect you. If I stay like this, nothing would have power to destroy me and I might generate greater powers to protect you," he told Michael.

Michael repeated his order loudly and then walked away from Lee.

"Look, don't you walk away from me like that!" Lee ran and stood in front of him. "I want you to understand that this could be our chance and we may not have this opportunity again. I want you to think about your decision before you regret this," Lee pleaded.

"You're copping out, Lee." Michael slipped through him and went to sit by Marizama. He couldn't believe his only friend from Thorn Valley was shirking his responsibility, not only toward him but also toward the group. What would his parents say when he came home from Thorn Valley without his friend's body?

Suddenly, a group of men wearing long black robes with a bright light around them came toward Lee. Some began attacking him while others went into the bedroom. Lee followed them and saw they were trying to escape through the window with his body.

"Put my body down!" Lee screamed. Michael heard it and wanted to run toward the bedroom, but Marizama stopped him and asked him to leave Lee alone. He sat back watching the door.

Lee let out a scream that echoed through the house. The men dropped his body and fled through the open window. He walked around his body to examine it, when he looked out the window and saw group of people, both men and women, standing and gazing at the window.

"There are no men in Texdulonicram. Where am I?" Lee asked.

He tried to pull his body to the bed, but his hand kept slipping through it, so he lay down on top of it. At that moment, Lee's soul penetrated his body like smoke entering through tiny holes. After a few minutes, he got up and walked to the dining room again. Michael stared at him. The girls looked on curiously. He then began to touch himself to feel his skin. It was back to normal.

Lee went back to the bedroom and glanced through the window; people were still gathered and gazing at him. They had long, white feather wings attached to their backs and began flying away one at the time.

"Strange place." Lee shook his head. He closed the window and turned back to Michael and the others. When Michael saw him, he ran and lightly touched him, making sure he was okay before he embraced him.

"How do you feel now?" Michael asked, smiling.

"I'm feeling fine. No pain or anything," he replied.

"Wonderful! Let's eat," said Marizama.

They all sat around the table ready to eat. The food was already served on their plates.

Azashema noticed a baked meat in one of the bowls. She asked Marizama about it because they were vegetarians.

"Oh, I prepared it for those humans," She pointed to Michael and Lee, who were ecstatic to be eating a well-cooked meal.

Lee took the fork and knife and tried to cut through the meat, but suddenly he saw that it had an ugly, tiny human head like a baby and was crying, "Ah! He wants to eat me!"

Lee fell backward from his chair, throwing the fork and knife up in the air.

Michael quickly lifted him up saying, "What's the matter with you?"

"Are you all right?" Marizama asked.

"Do I look all right to you? Didn't you see what just happened?"

"Not at all," Michael answered.

Lee began describing what he saw, and Azashema began to chuckle.

"You did this, didn't you?" Lee asked her.

"No," she said, quickly becoming straight-faced.

Michael and the others wanted to crack up, but since Lee stared at them frustrated, they stopped. He and Michael exchanged plates. Lee watched Michael eat his meat vigorously.

When they were finished eating, Michael called Lee aside and asked him again, "Are you sure you're okay, or is there something bothering you that you're trying to hide from me?"

"Look, Michael. I'm not crazy! I told you what I saw. You just have to believe me." They dropped that topic.

The next morning, all the residents of Texdulonicram were gathered at the stadium waiting for the boys. Michael and the group woke up, got dressed, and asked Marizama to accompany them.

"Come on, guys. Hurry! People are waiting. I will sit among the crowd, and I will find you when the meeting is over," Marizama promised.

"Why are they waiting for us? We only told them to find themselves a leader," Michael said.

"I don't know myself. Anyway, we don't have much time left."

"I don't want them to see us like celebrities and start chasing after us. I have enough of that at home," said Michael.

"Stop asking too many questions, Michael. When we are done, you can ask all the questions you want," Azashema told him. They grabbed his hand and walked to the stadium.

When the audience saw the boys, they went wild. Joan pushed Michael to the front of the area to face the crowd, but he came back and asked, "What should I say?"

"Say anything you want; we will support you," Joan told him. He moved fearfully ahead and saw everybody watching him.

"Have you people found yourself a leader yet?" he asked in a squeaky voice.

An old woman walked to the front and suggested that he should be their leader.

"You need a woman to lead you. Lee and I don't belong here; we have to go back to Thorn Valley. We only came here to help destroy Azamerie, the sorceress."

But the same old woman repeated, "We don't want another leader, but you!" The audience applauded loudly.

They were shouting his name. He couldn't say another word because the audience was chanting his name too loudly. He walked back to his friends. Joan told him to stay back. She went in front. As soon as they saw her, they quieted down to hear what she had to say.

"I think you got this wrong! These boys are not from this kingdom. They have done you all a great favor. They have to go back to the real world in Livingstone. They have no intention of being your leaders!"

"What do you mean they're from the real world? This is the real world! Are you trying to tell us we aren't good enough for Michael to rule?" the same old lady asked.

Michael walked toward the woman. "Please, tell us your name?"

"My name is Cathrizama Milode, and I was chosen by these people to communicate with you."

"I'm not trying to tell you that we're better than you in any way. Seeing that you have so much confidence in me, I will meet you here at this time tomorrow. I will think very hard about a solution to this matter," he said.

"Make sure you really do some thinking about this situation, because we don't have time to come here every day," Cathrizama warned. She turned and dismissed the crowd.

"I'll have to find a way to escape from this kingdom as quickly as possible, before they turn against me. I can't be their leader," Michael told his friends as they circled around him.

"All right, let's go home and think how we can handle this," Marizama suggested.

After they went back to Marizama's house, Michael asked Lee to stroll with him outside in the garden.

"Sorry you had to find yourself in the middle of this matter. If I had known, we wouldn't have allowed you to go out there in the first place," Lee said.

"Actually, it wasn't anyone's fault, and I can't hold anyone responsible. I guess it's just how it's supposed to be. My father always tells me that nothing happens for nothing. I believe there is a reason for this," Michael said.

"Are you telling me you want to stay here for the rest of your life? Don't forget that the citizens of Livingstone are wholly relying on you when your father is gone. Your life is in Livingstone and not here," Lee said.

"Wait a minute. Do you think I want to throw away my kingship? No way. I'm thinking how to get out of here before something goes wrong. Have any ideas?"

"I have been thinking, but I haven't really found a way out yet."

"Can you call Joan and Azashema?"

"Why?" Lee asked.

"Will you just call them?" Michael commanded.

Lee did. They came and sat by him on the white bench in the manicured garden. Pink and red gardenias covered the green lawn.

"Beautiful, isn't it?" said Joan, looking around.

"Yes," agreed Azashema. They turned to look at the boys and listened attentively as Michael began speaking.

"First of all, I want to thank you two for your kindness. I hope one day we will be able to repay you."

"You don't have to worry. We're friends now. Anyway, you seem to have something on your mind you want to share with us," Azashema said.

"Yes. Do you know a way out of here, back to the Kingdom of Livingstone?"

"The only way we know will take you several weeks. That means you will have to be traveling rapidly because this city is far from land," Joan said.

"If you leave here, you will pass through the deep dark water filled with tough currents. It will take a week to get straight to the top. We can't assure your safety because it's another creature's territory, and besides, the current within the dark waters could blow your eardrums in seconds, killing you instantly. The creatures that live there have never been discovered by man, and they don't want to see any other living creature around them. So you guys should think about this thoroughly and make up your minds," Azashema added.

"How old did you tell us you were?" Michael asked.

"Why do you ask?"

"I want to know. When I grow up, I pray to meet a woman as beautiful and as smart as you and your sister," Michael said.

"Yes, we know; you told us," they chuckled. "We are ninety-seven years old in Texdulonicram years, and we are twin sisters. When you calculate that in human terms, it would come up to twelve years old. That's why we said we were twelfths," Joan answered.

"In my kingdom, when you see a ninety-seven-year-old person, they're very old. It's hard for people to reach that age. If you had asked me how old you were, I would have said eleven or twelve," Michael said, smiling.

"Ouch! Are you serious?" Joan asked.

"Yes, I am."

"You're so sweet. No wonder this city wants you to lead them," she said, and they laughed.

Lee rose and started to pace. "Guys, listen to this. I was just thinking about our situation," he began. They stopped and turned to him. "I think it's great that they squeezed Michael into this situation."

"What are you talking about?" Azashema asked raising her eyebrows.

"Michael, you told me earlier that everything happens for a reason, which is true. I don't think we should run away from this. We have to do something about their request. I think we already have the answer to their demand."

"What do you mean? Go straight to the point, Lee!" Michael said, watching his friend walk from one side to the other.

"These sisters are the answer. They will stay here and lead them," Lee answered.

"Who told you we want to be leaders?" Azashema asked furiously.

"You girls are the same as they are and from the same part of the world. With your strength and knowledge, you'll give them exactly what they want, which is freedom," Lee answered.

"I think you're going out of your mind and need to be checked!" Joan said as they walked away, whispering to each other.

A New Leader

Michael stared at Lee and shook his head in disappointment.

"We're men; we think and understand things differently from women. This time, you went overboard. I'll leave it to you to fix it," Michael said.

"I was only trying to help out. I never thought it would turn out this way. I didn't mean to offend them. I just thought they would be a good match for the job." Lee turned to look at his friend. "Trust me, Michael, I'll talk to them and patch things up."

Lee went inside and called Marizama. Together, they strolled into the garden as Michael went inside to rest.

"Do you think you have a future in this city?" Lee asked Marizama as she bent to smell one of the gardenias.

"Why are you asking me such a question?"

"Just curious." He bent alongside her.

"Well, I think this is a wonderful city. I love everything about it. So, yes, I intend to stay here," she answered, rising.

"Can you tell me the one thing you love most about this city?" Lee followed her lead.

"When I first came to this city from my hometown, Xludosen, I saw a big difference." She stopped and looked at Lee. "You see, in my hometown there are both males and females, and sometimes we were forced into a relationship by the king's order. But here nobody cares who you are, which is great. I think Azamerie was too tough on the residents, forcing them into her dogma, and so everyone learned to mind their own business."

"There's one more question." Lee watched as Marizama picked a stray leaf from one of the plants. "Do you think Joan and Azashema can take over for Azamerie?"

"To be honest, I think they're terrific, and they're both very intelligent."

"Thank you. I appreciate your answers."

"Glad I could help," Marizama said, looking at Lee curiously.

Lee went back into the house to talk to Azashema, but she refused to go anywhere without her sister.

"Okay, bring her," Lee told her.

The girls followed him outside into the garden. Marizama watched them from the kitchen window.

"I apologize for what happened earlier."

"We forgive you," Azashema said with her eyes wide open.

"There's something I want to ask you both." Lee led them to the bench. "Do you love this city?"

"Yes," they answered.

"How long have you been living here?"

"We don't live here. We only came for the competition," Azashema answered curtly.

"Look here, ladies. Michael is in serious trouble. We have to help him, and I think you girls are the only people who can. You girls are beautiful and smart—the perfect combination."

"Yes, we know! You told us this before, and we are actually tired of hearing it. Look, you have to tell us why you called us here because we want to get some rest," Azashema said rudely, wearing an impatient frown.

Lee blushed and then smiled forcibly, trying to be as tactful as possible. "I appreciate you both coming."

"Is this what you called us here for?" Joan asked angrily.

"Yes," Lee replied, hoping he could vanish beneath the earth.

They walked away, looking at him as if he were crazy.

Michael walked outside to sit on the bench with Lee. "You have to help me out here, because those girls are getting more wrathful by the second."

"What do you want me to tell them?" Michael asked, pushing his hair back off his forehead.

"It's simple. The people of this city will be happy with your verdict. Talk to the girls, and tell them to accept the position. I have a bad feeling about this entire thing. If we don't find solutions now, we will be in big trouble tomorrow. We have to use our brains to get out of here alive," Lee said apprehensively. "Azamerie might still have some of her most trusted servants searching for revenge."

"My father told me that decision makers think long and hard about their decisions. The more you sit and think, the more ideas you acquire. Do you think I want to stay here another minute? I want to get back to Thorn Valley as quickly as possible—even more than you do. Follow me," Michael said. As they walked inside, Michael yelled out, "I can't do it!"

"Do what?" Marizama asked as the boys walked by the kitchen.

"Be their leader! I have a personal obligation to attend to at Thorn Valley."

"Is there something you want to share with us?" she asked Michael.

"Yes."

"Then sit down," she said. They sat down at the kitchen table.

"I will only be able to convince this city if I find somebody capable of ruling them," Michael said.

Marizama turned to Azashema and her sister, who came through the door to join in the conversation. They pulled up a chair and sat at the bright yellow table.

"Do you girls want to stay here with us in this beautiful city?" Marizama asked.

"No! Our city is ten times better than this! Besides, we're entertainers. We love to travel the world. We are leaders in our field, and we love it. I know why you asked," Joan said, grinning at Lee.

"Wait a minute! You live here, Marizama. Why don't you take the job?" Joan asked.

"That's a great idea! You will be saving all of us," Lee said.

"Like I said, I love this city, and I want to stay here for the rest of my life. So, if you guys think I'm qualified for this job, I'll accept it."

"Sure! You are qualified. From our little conversations, I know you can do anything. My father told me that bad things happen all the time, but good things come once in a while. When good thing comes, you have to take it and make use of it." Michael stood up, walked over to Marizama, and put his hands on her shoulders.

"Your father says a lot of interesting things, doesn't he?" said Marizama.

Michael nodded and said to Marizama, "I believe you are a good person. You know why?" He turned his head to look directly at her. "You took us in and treated us like kings and queens. How much more kindness can a stranger anticipate? This city will love you," Michael said confidently.

"Thank you," she said.

"Now, in case they refuse my decision, you girls should back me up. Help me make them accept my decision and respect it." The girls agreed.

"Well, I think this problem is solved. Thank you, my dear friends," Lee said. He got up and strolled outside; Michael followed.

"Have you noticed something about yourself lately?" Michael asked.

"What?"

"I'm talking about your complexion."

"What about it?"

"It's getting fairer."

"Are you serious?" Lee asked in astonishment.

"Yes, I am!"

Lee laughed. "I am not rich, but I still have lots of diamonds and other precious stones with me," he reminded Michael.

"Keep them. They just saved our lives. Maybe they will help us in the future," Michael said.

"Let's go and sit with the women." They walked back into the bright square kitchen.

"It's a beautiful day. We should do something for fun," Lee suggested, walking toward the table.

"What do you have in mind?" Azashema asked.

"I was thinking we should go for a walk around the neighborhood to get to know the area instead of sitting here doing nothing."

"That's a good idea," Joan responded happily.

"Wait here. Let me change into something more suitable," Marizama said and went to her room.

Michael drew his friends together and explained what had happened when he was with Marizama earlier. The girls were stunned.

"She always pretends to be innocent!" Azashema said.

"Come and take a look." They swiftly followed him into the hallway, but it wasn't the way Michael had described it, so they began to laugh and tease him.

"Good imagination, Michael," Lee chuckled.

"Stop laughing; I'm telling the truth!"

"We believe you. Come on, let's go back before she thinks we're all into her business," Azashema said. They sat on the gray sofa in the living room and waited for Marizama.

When Marizama was ready, they all got up and followed her. They passed by manicured front lawns adorned with sprinkling fountains in front of looming homes in various shapes and sizes. No two homes looked the same. They looked around curiously, and then began to compare the different kingdoms.

"What are the most expensive natural resources that are commonly used in this kingdom?" Michael asked Marizama.

"It's different here. We don't value mineral resources in this city because they're not rare. The only thing people care about is freedom. What about Livingstone?"

"We value precious stones. Diamonds, gold, and other precious stones are expensive in Livingstone," Lee answered, shaking the diamonds in his pocket.

"We have them everywhere in the streets. As you walk, just look down. You'll find them in all sizes."

"There's a place in the north end of this city where an entire mountain is gold, and nobody cares. People just pass it by. If you want, I can take you there right now," Marizama suggested.

"I think it would be great to see," Lee said.

"Okay. Let's cross to the other side and take a bus."

* * * * *

When they arrived at the mountain, it was huge and pure gold. It had no grass or soil around it. But, as Michael and Lee walked around, Marizama warned that it was forbidden to go close to it or to touch it. "If you do, you will have a great curse placed upon you and your families' heads."

"Nonsense! Gold is gold. They just told you that to scare you off, so you don't try to cut into it and take some with you. You girls stay here. Lee and I will tour around it a little," Michael said.

"Okay, but don't be long. If you need help, just scream our names," Azashema said.

The mountain shone gold as the warm sun radiated its rays above it. It was beautiful; they had never seen anything like it before. Broken pieces of rugged gold around the mountain reflected light. Lee severed a piece, looked at it closely, and then put it in his pocket, along with the diamonds.

The ground started to vibrate, and green lights flashed from every corner of the mountain.

"What on earth did you do?" Michael screamed. "Put that piece back!"

Lee tried to take the piece back out of his pocket, but the earth quaked so hard, he wobbled, lost his balance, and fell.

"I think we should get out of here because a large piece of this gold could break off and hit us on the head and kill us," Michael yelled out, trying to take a step, but he flipped back onto the ground.

"There's nowhere to run. We have to stay right here until things settle down!" Lee said.

The vibrations from the mountain affected the entire city. People could see the flashing lights from every angle. Michael and Lee heard faint screams as residents ran for cover.

All of a sudden, the sky dimmed over the horizon. The entire kingdom blackened. Michael and Lee heard the girls screaming their names.

"We're here. Over here!" Michael said as the vibrating earth slowed.

"What happened?" Azashema called out. Darkness made it hard to see as they stepped cautiously nearer to the mountain.

"Lee here decided he wanted some gold to add to his diamond collection," Michael yelled, laughing.

After an hour, the green lights started to slowly go off, and the darkness began clearing, restoring daylight. Azashema and her sister walked closer to the mountain.

"Don't touch it, whatever you do," said Joan.

"Here they are," Azashema told her sister as they saw the boys leaning against the mountain. "Are you guys all right?"

"Yes, we think so," Lee answered as he felt along his arms and legs. "No broken bones."

While they were talking, Joan told them to keep silent and look up in the direction her finger was pointing. A long ladder leading from the mountaintop sprang down toward the ground.

"I knew there was something about this mountain. Gold normally melts at high heat, but this gold produces high heat and withstand it," Michael said.

"What are you trying to say?" Lee asked.

Just then, Marizama appeared from behind a bush. "To tell you the truth, I don't think the residents of this kingdom have experienced a blackout like this in a long time. Everyone knows about the curse and is careful not to try and cut a piece off the mountain."

"Well, I don't believe in the curse, because we touched it and nothing happened. It's only when I cut off a piece that the earth started to vibrate," Lee said.

"You can walk around, I guess, but don't start taking any of the gold with you," Marizama said.

"Marizama, tell us what's on the other side," Michael asked.

"I think Livingstone is on the other side," she replied.

"Livingstone? I think it's time to head home."

"Not before you tell the people who their new leader will be this afternoon."

"Can't you tell them? We appreciate everything you've done for us, but I really think I should be getting home now. Lee, let's go," Michael said.

"Michael, you're a cop-out. You promised you'd find them a leader, and now you're backing out."

"I did find them a leader—you." Michael became angry. "Look, Marizama, I've been waiting to get home for a long time, and I think it's time to get going. I'm sure my parents are wondering about me, since I haven't been in touch for so long."

"Wait a minute! Look at the height of this thing. It will take us many hours to get up there," Lee told him.

"Well, if you never try, you'll never know."

"Michael is right. I think there's something important up there. That's why this ladder has arrived to take you there," Azashema agreed.

"How do you know this ladder isn't a death trap?" Lee asked in a shrill voice.

"We take risks every day. We are going to go up there with Michael. If you want, you can stay down here with Marizama," Azashema told him. "Besides, I want to see Michael's palace."

Joan nodded in agreement. "We'll come back and let you know what we saw on the other side, Marizama."

"Okay. I'll wait for you, Joan."

"I'll go up with Michael," said Lee. "Don't mind me; sometimes I get too insecure about safety. But to be honest, my insecurity has actually saved my life on many occasions," he said.

"Come on, guys. Let's go," Michael said.

They started climbing up the rungs of the ladder one by one. It was a long way up, and it took almost three hours to get to the middle of the mountain where Michael saw a huge door with large golden handles.

"What do you want to do?" Joan asked.

"I was thinking we should go inside to rest for a while before continuing," Michael said.

The Gold Mountain Trap

"**C**ome on, guys. It's empty in here," Michael called out after he entered through the door. The girls followed.

"This is the first time I've entered a room of pure gold. This is like a dream," Michael said.

Lee was looking around in an adjacent room when he spotted another gold door. "Guys, take a look at this!" Michael and the girls went into the room.

"Open it!" Azashema said.

"I think we should just stay right here and leave that door alone," Lee warned as his insecurity got the best of him again.

"I think he's right; we should stick to the plan," Michael added.

Joan moved in front of the door. Her sister followed. "Are you guys coming inside with us or not?" she asked.

"You really want us to go in there?" Lee's fingers began to quiver.

She glanced at his scared face and laughed. "Yes!" she answered.

"We have to work as a team." Michael passed Lee as he slowly walked toward the girls. As future king, he had to practice courage.

"I will count from one to three, and then I will open it at once," Joan said. "One, two three …"

The room was dark. As soon as they entered, the door slammed behind them, and the room began lighting up. The sudden light almost blinded them, making it difficult to see anything around them. They held onto each other as the illumination normalized. They began to hear noises behind them. They all turned and saw a large, open room crammed with wild and aggressive creatures in the shape of men. The creatures had long tails and claws resembling dogs and lion noses; however, they behaved like cavemen. The creatures in the front row were giants, dressed in human attire. They frown grinding their teeth hard, as if they were ready to rupture the boys and girls.

"Okay, nobody panic. We should all stick together and watch them closely," Michael whispered. There looked to be three to four thousands creatures.

"I think this kind of creature is called a Vasfere," Azashema said. "I've seen them before. I think they are one of Azamerie's creations."

After a couple of minutes, the Vasferes began to push closer, as though getting ready to attack. Michael and his friends slowly pulled themselves back against the wall. When Michael looked behind him to open the door, he realized that the door had vanished.

The Vasferes approached and stood close to the four of them, furiously grinding their teeth. Michael walked calmly to the front and stared at them.

"We regret bothering you," Michael began, "but if you show us the door, we will leave, and you will never see us again."

At this, the huge Vasferes started barking at them like dogs. One of them aggressively grabbed Azashema's shirt and tore off the sleeve. She began to scream, but Michael told her to keep calm.

"Please, don't argue back. I don't care how strong we are; we can't subdue them. Look at them; there are thousands in here."

"There's no door," Lee fearfully reminded them.

"We can see that. Where were you when I said earlier that the doors were gone?" Azashema ask him.

"Why are you always picking on me?" he asked her.

"I'm not. I'm just telling you to keep your eyes wide and watchful; that's all. Be alert, especially in a situation like this."

Lee furiously glared at her without a word. Michael asked them to keep silent.

"You guys should have listened to me before we went up the ladder. Now we're going to die," Lee cried.

"Be quiet!" the other three said in unison.

Suddenly, one of the Vasferes grabbed Joan by the leg and dragged her among the multitudes of Vasferes. As they were about to disseminate her, they heard a deep grinding voice shouting, "Everyone, stop!"

The creatures immediately released her, and she ran back to her friends. The four of them quickly started searching for where the voice had come from.

"I told them to stop," a youth said in a human voice as he walked to the front and glared at them. His brown eyes peered out from an animal-like face covered with a full head of spiky brown hair. He was the same height as Lee.

"My name is Patrick. I know you heard me. You've entered the wrong kingdom. This is the Kingdom of Warsmost, and they call us Vasferes."

Michael nodded as he continued. "Now you have nowhere to run. If you want to know about magic, you have come to the right place, because I invented it. Do you know what I'm going to do with you?" he asked.

"Eat us?" Michael asked.

"We're villainous. I will allow my boys to hang you up on that long pole behind me. We'll slash you little by little with our razor-sharp claws then watch you die in pain. Now, when you talk about pain, I invented it," Patrick said.

Patrick sauntered around and smelled Michael's feet; he glared at him, licking his mouth. Suddenly, all the Vasferes started licking their mouths hungrily.

"What's your name, young man?" Patrick asked.

"Me?" Michael asked.

"You, just stand there and shut up! I already know who you are. I am talking to your friend over there."

"Oh, sorry. My name is Lee. And you are Patrick?"

"Don't worry about me. I can see you kids are four in number. I need a boy and a girl. I'll give you twenty seconds to choose among yourselves."

"What do you want to do with them?" Michael asked anxiously.

"I can see you ask lots of questions, and I know your friends told you this before. Either you give me what I've asked for, or I'll take what I want by force. You have ten more seconds."

Patrick's eyes grew red, and his hair stood up as the other fearsome Vasferes stood by, prepared and anxious for his command.

"Look, guys. We're not giving anyone up to that animal. I say we stick together," Joan muttered.

"I agree, but we have to scare them off when they attempt to ambush us. We should prove our superiority to them as humans," Michael whispered.

Patrick waited calmly for the seconds to end to see what they would do. The group continued whispering in a huddle. When time was up, Patrick spoke to his men in a language their prey didn't understand. At once, the Vasferes grabbed all of them by their legs and dragged them into another large, empty room. Patrick stepped on a little button, and the floor suddenly opened right under them. They fell into a little basement. He stepped back on the button, and the area closed up, leaving them trapped in the dark.

"What happen to the magic you had? Why didn't you use it?" Michael asked Azashema.

"You shouldn't talk like that because we're all magicians, and you could have used yours," Azashema corrected him.

"Guys, shut up and think!" Lee yelled out. They kept quiet.

After a couple of seconds, they realized that Michael wasn't among them. They couldn't believe he had used his magic to save himself and left them there to die. The girls tried using their magic, but it wouldn't work, so they became angry at Lee.

"Extricate us from this place!" they screamed.

"Listen to me for a second; Michael never goes anyplace without me. Since we're all in this situation and he's not here, that means something isn't right. Maybe they used their magic to steal him away. I remember Patrick telling him that he knew who he was. Michael is too loyal to leave us. I beg you, stay calm," Lee pleaded.

They sat in silence. The sisters sat by themselves while Lee sat in the far corner, looking sad.

Meanwhile, Patrick was holding Michael. He told him, "I know who you are, and I know you're here not by your own will. You have come for a good purpose, and I appreciate it. You have come here to die." As Patrick spoke, he was transforming into a human, back to himself.

"Who are you?" Michael asked.

"We're human men. Many years ago, we were happily living with our families, like you do in your kingdom. Azamerie self-ishly showed up and transmogrified us.

"She kept us here because she never wanted men to mingle with women, so she transmogrified our way of life, our women, and every value we have ever lived for. We got the news that you've exterminated her, but I tell you, she never dies. She just retreats to get prepared; she will be back."

"I don't think so. We made sure she was completely dead." Michael explained what had happened.

"Listen to me, young man. I know the person we're talking about. She might even be in Kshuludiom right now as we speak," Patrick said.

"So what do you want me to do? What do you want from me?"

"That's an excellent question. I know you are the Prince of Livingstone, and your parents are very wealthy. You have come a long way, and I'm delighted you have come this far. We've been stuck in here for ages. We need a way to break free, and only you can help us. That's why we called you here. Look at us; do you think we're animals? We are men!"

"Is that why, when you speak, your face suddenly transmogrifies into a human's?"

"I don't know." Patrick scratched his head.

"Now listen to me, you have my friends down there. Set them free and make them as comfortable as I am, because without them I will not be able to help you."

Quickly, Patrick brought them all back upstairs and apologized for the misunderstanding. They were excited to see Michael, who explained what had happened.

"These men have been in prison for centuries. They want to be humans again. They want to go back as humans to their wives and children in Texdulonicram. They want to be free, and we're their only hope," Michael said. "The evil Azamerie wanted only her kind in her kingdom. She wanted complete control, and so she changed these men's lives forever."

"That's scary and evil," said Lee. "You mean she destroyed whole families?"

"Yes."

"Do the women know these men are still alive?" Azashema asked.

"I don't think so," Michael answered. "We have to help them get back to their wives and children."

"We'll do what we can to help," said Joan.

Joan walked back to Patrick and told him that they were willing to help.

"I already heard it all."

Azashema came toward Patrick and asked, "What do you feed on in here?"

71

"Nothing. Since we've arrived here, we haven't tasted food. We don't have any appetite; we're always full."

"How many of you have died since you came here?" Lee asked, coming closer to join the conversation.

"None, but we can't get outside. When we try to pass through that second door, a strong light like lightning fires from nowhere and strikes us hard, forcefully throwing us back inside; the door vanishes as it did for you. This has kept us stuck in here for years. We don't know where our wives or children are."

"Why did all these giants choose you as their leader?" Lee asked.

"Because I'm the strongest. In here, you need somebody like me to keep the peace."

"You are too short. What kind of strength do you have which those other men don't?" Lee asked.

"I was a magician. Besides, I'm very powerful when it comes to protecting them; it has been like this with me since I was born. I've always been a leader, even before we were thrown here by Azamerie. But I can't get us out, nor change us back to humans."

"But if you have all this magic power, why did you allow Azamerie to disgrace you this way?" Michael asked.

"All magical powers are not equal. Azamerie was a strong sorceress. When she arrived in our kingdom, she demanded that everybody follow and worship her tradition and her command. The men rose up against her, and that's why she changed us into Vasferes and hid us in here where no one has ever found us. She destroyed my life and the lives of all the men in here," Patrick said.

"If you knew who we were, why were you risking your lives by threatening us?" Joan asked.

"We only knew Michael. One of the Vasferes recognized him from Livingstone and knows he is a prince."

"Since we've been in here, nobody has ever entered through that door before," Patrick said. "So we were just protecting ourselves, in case you wanted to harm us."

"Patrick, let us go and prepare a plan to help you," Michael said.

"How do I know you will come back?"

"You have my word as the Prince of Livingstone."

"Then your word is good. Go, and come back soon so that we can reunite with our families."

Leaving the Animal Kingdom

young Vasfere anxiously ran before them, and they followed through the rooms of the mountain. It took them two hours to get back to where they entered. There was no door. They knocked around on the walls, trying to locate a way out as the Vasferes watched them.

"Wait, guys, why are we doing this?" Joan said. "Move back, and close your ears!"

They did. Joan and her sister pointed their hands at the walls, and a red-hot light flashed from their fingers like a red laser beam. The light was so powerful and hot that the Vasferes moved far back while Lee and Michael stood nearby, wiping the sweat from their faces. As the girls moved their fingers, the fire from the hot beam quickly spread in little portions, cutting right through the walls to form the shape of a door. Thick pieces of gold fell as the floor vibrated.

"Come on, guys," the sisters called. They waved good-bye to the Vasferes, slipped into the next room, and finally spotted the sunlight.

The group walked to the ladder and climbed fast for an hour to reach the top. In Livingstone, his father could help him find a solution for the Vasferes, Michael thought. Although the kingdoms didn't usually interfere with each other's affairs, this was a special case, and Michael knew his father would help him find a solution to the problem. The mountaintop was flat and clean, but the far left was white with snow and a cold breeze was blowing from there.

"Let's search everywhere before retreating," Michael suggested.

"What are we looking for?" Lee asked.

"For a way back to Livingstone. Marizama said that this is the way there," Michael said.

"She said she *thought* this was the way to Livingstone. She didn't say she was sure," Joan said.

After minutes of searching, they saw nothing but pieces of broken gold everywhere. Michael didn't give up. He had to find a way to Livingstone to solicit his father's help. He continued walking until he suddenly came across a ladder leading down to a large gold door.

"Look!" Michael pointed.

They quickly ran to look. Lee walked behind them reluctantly. "So, what do you want us to do?" he asked.

"Go investigate," Michael answered.

"I think we should get away from this area. A bad feeling came over me when I looked down there."

The girls glared at him and suspected he was scared.

"If you're scared, then why don't you stay here and wait so we can check it out quickly? You never know; there might be another exit, which may take us straight to Livingstone," Joan predicted.

Lee looked around in all four directions anxiously and then said, "No, I think I'll come with you." He held onto Michael's arm.

"Let's get moving!" Michael said.

As soon as they all stepped on the ladder, they suddenly found themselves in a wide, open area at the bottom of the mountain. Michael collapsed and passed out. After a minute, he woke up and gave out a loud yell.

"He's alive! He's alive!" Lee shouted.

"What happened? Are you all right?" Azashema asked anxiously.

He opened his eyes and saw Lee kneeling above him with tears rolling from his eyes.

"Is that you, Lee?" Michael asked.

"Yes, it's me."

"Where are the others?"

"They're all here."

"Are you all right?" Joan asked.

"I don't know."

They sat around and advised him to rest a little. After a couple of minutes, Michael stood up and stared at them.

"What happened to you?" Azashema asked again.

"This isn't a good place. I think Patrick was right, because I saw Azamerie. I think she's still alive some place in this mountain. I say we get out of here as quickly as possible," he warned them.

"We've tried searching everywhere to locate an exit, but all we found was forest to the left and desert to the right, and it's so hot out there," Lee said.

"But we must get out of here!" Michael warned.

"Okay, calm down," Azashema said. "What was she doing when you saw her in your vision?"

"She aggressively attacked us and immediately bit the three of you to death. After that, she slashed my head off with her long, razor-sharp fingernails, and I had it in my hand, screaming, before I woke up."

"Are you strong enough to walk?" Azashema asked.

"Very strong."

"Then I think we should go, but which way? Through the desert or through the forest?" she asked.

"Through the desert," Michael suggested.

They made their way out into the sunlit expanse and began trudging slowly through the yellowish grains that looked like sand.

"This doesn't look like sand to me," Lee said.

"What are you talking about?" Michael asked.

Lee bent over and took some into his palm.

"It looks like gold dust to me," Michael said. "Put that down before all of Texdulonicram starts to shake again." Lee threw the dust onto the ground.

They continued walking. They didn't notice that the more they lingered in the desert, the hotter the gold dust became. Lee fell into the gold and began to roll in it as the girls stood by, staring at him and laughing. He got up and shook the gold off his clothes. He took some, threw it in the air, and it suddenly spread into a big circle.

"Look!" he pointed.

When they turned, they saw a circle of shiny clean gold. Within five seconds, an image appeared in it. They quickly ran closer to watch. The image stopped forming, and the gold scattered and fell.

They turned to Lee. "What did you do?"

He began explaining, but as he demonstrated, the same big circle formed. An image appeared. It was Marizama.

"Can you guys hear me?" she asked from the circle.

"Yes, we can hear you loud and clear!" Michael said.

"I waited at the spot where you left me for hours, and I got tired and came home. Where are you now?"

"We're in an area that appears to be a desert of gold, and we're walking through it right now. There are no buildings or trees around here, so we're wondering what kind of place this is," Joan said.

"Okay. Give me couple of minutes. I will check it out, and you can call me by using the same method," she said. Her image vanished from the circle. She appeared in the circle again after they called her.

"Hello!" she called out.

"Yes, we can hear you!" Michael said.

"Please! You guys should turn right now and run from that entire area back to the cave. Carry a handful of gold dust with you. A volcano erupted ahead of you, and it's speeding toward you. It's melting all the gold!" she warned in a strong voice. "You won't make it to Livingstone. The pathway is blocked with gold lava."

"Thank you very much. Guys, we've got to go!" Joan said.

They turned in the opposite direction and start running. After a minute, they started to feel the intense heat and ran faster. They looked behind and saw a thick orange fire spreading quickly. Gold dust ran like rivers of water. The heat was approaching closer than they had expected.

"Run! Run!" Michael screamed. Lee tripped over his feet, and Michael ran back and picked him up.

"We have a long way to go. You've got to take care of yourself, buddy, because I love you." Michael was gasping hard.

"The Prince of Livingstone loves me."

"No time for joking. Let's go!" Michael screamed.

"I'm not joking. I love you too … like a brother," Lee said breathlessly.

The sisters were far ahead and didn't look back.

"Faster, Lee, I won't leave you behind!" Michael yelled, turning his head to his friend.

Joan and Azashema were getting close to the cave, while Michael and Lee were still trying to catch up. They were soaked with sweat as the melted gold slid closer. They caught up with the girls and stopped to catch their breath. They entered the cave.

Michael stood at the mouth and asked, "Did anyone bring some gold dust?"

"No, we forgot," they answered.

"Wait here; I'll get some," Michael ran outside, but the melted gold was almost at the door of the cave, and the heat was unbearable. Michael grabbed a handful, even though it was searing hot. He removed his wallet and dropped the gold dust inside. Then he ran back to the cave as Lee screamed at him to hurry.

As soon as Michael sprang inside the cave, the melted gold flowed around and covered the cave entirely. They stayed locked up in the sweltering heat until the following morning. The thick, heavy gold buried the cave, and they were trapped inside. Hungry and exhausted, they started pacing, trying to think of a way to get out.

"Where is the gold dust?" Lee asked Michael.

Michael tried to empty his wallet, but in it, there was one solid piece of gold and a few small pieces. He carefully placed them in Lee's palm. The girls asked him to throw it up in the air. Maybe Marizama would come into a screen and tell them how to get out of the cave. Lee flipped the stones into the air, but they came down and scattered all over the place in a way that made it impossible to pick them up. There was no gold dust and no way out. The four of them sat on the floor, thinking.

Michael got up and started walking around. He saw a sparkle on the earth beneath him and quickly put his hand on it. It was gold dust that the wind had blown into the cave earlier. He searched for more and located a small mound.

"I found some!" he yelled. The others bent down beside him as he lifted his arm into the air and threw the gold dust upwards. They watched it slowly transform, bringing light into the cave. As soon the circle was formed, Marizama appeared.

"I can see you are trapped, but it's better than dying out in the heat."

"Thank you for warning us," Michael said.

"Don't worry about it. I checked my map, and the exit on your right is the only way out. It will take you down to the ground, and you won't have to go outside or down the ladder," Marizama said.

They looked right, but saw nothing.

"Can't see an exit," Michael told her.

"Push the gold out of the way. It will open easily."

They pushed at the location Marizama indicated, and the solid gold rolled out of the way, leading them to a golden staircase. The stairs were wide enough, and they began descending. As they were going down, Michael remembered Marizama. He ran back and saw her still waiting.

"Thank you. We've found the way. We'll meet you in Texdulonicram soon."

"Okay. I will pick you up right in front of the mountain. Don't forget to remove this circle."

He did so and then followed the others, who were waiting for him on the stairs.

"Let's go," he said. They descended the stairs for what seemed like hours, resting occasionally on one of the steps. When they finally reached the ground, it was already dark.

"Over here! I'm here!" they heard a familiar voice calling out to them.

When they turned, they saw Marizama waving at them. They ran across the road and hugged her, thanking her for saving their lives. She told them to get into the car. They dozed on the drive home.

The next morning, they awoke early and waited in the living room for Marizama to awaken.

"We're leaving for a couple of hours. We are traveling to our magic professor to find solutions for Patrick's problems," Azashema said.

"Can we come with you to make sure you're safe? We can also give you a helping hand with your work," Lee suggested.

"That's so sweet, but where we're going, you can't follow. Anyway, we'll see you two soon. We won't be gone long," Azashema said.

"What should we tell Marizama when she wakes up?" Michael asked.

"Nothing," Azashema replied, and they swiftly vanished.

"Look, Lee. Those girls are only helping us. They're not our girl-friends or anything. Can you just allow me to do the talking next time? I don't know what is wrong with you lately; you've turned into a completely different person. You're too paranoid, and every-body can see it just by looking at you. When I met you, you were very brave. Look, most of the time, I only pretend to be brave, and it works like a charm." Michael sat beside him on the sofa. "You are the only one I trust, so we have to stick together. And please, behave like the guy I took you for. Think before you react," Michael advised him.

"I don't know what you're talking about," Lee said innocently.

"Use your mouth and your body language to make people believe you are capable of threatening them, and they might take you seriously."

"Good idea. I guess I've become a frightened, apologetic geek. Do you think those girls will come back?"

"Don't just rely on others to save you. Always have a backup plan in case the situation turns against you. Stay tough," Michael said. He looked at his friend, who seemed confused. "And yeah, they probably will come back. Don't worry; I have a plan," Michael said.

Touring with Marizama

"It's daylight, and Marizama isn't up yet. Are you sure she's all right?" Lee asked.

"I don't know; I think she's just tired. We had a long day yesterday. I want to stroll around the neighborhood a little," Michael said.

"I'll go with you." Lee rose after him. They walked to the door, which had a decorative stainless steel handle.

"Did you just see what I saw?" Michael asked.

"What?"

"The door handle moved as I was about to touch it."

"Move back so I can see," Lee said.

He grabbed the handle with both hands and suddenly realized his hands were stuck.

"It's getting hotter by the second. Michael, do something. It looks like I'm trapped here!"

"Stop playing around! Pull your hand off so I can open the door."

"I'm not joking. My hand is stuck, and I can feel the hot iron burning my palm. Please, do something quickly!" he cried.

Michael watched his face and saw him turning crimson. "Try opening your hand so I can pull you out!"

"I can't." His face began to look as if he was about to cry.

"Remember what I said—stay tough," Michael tried to pull him away from the door, but Lee felt heavier, and he was unable to move him.

"Call Marizama. Quickly!" Lee cried out.

"I'll go wake her up," Michael said, but as soon as he took his first step, he stumbled on the stairs and fell. He quickly rose, ran toward her door, and knocked, screaming her name.

"I'm right behind you," she said.

"Oh! I'm sorry. I thought you were still in bed."

"I was. I heard you calling. That is why I came out. Is everything all right?" She tied the belt around her teal satin robe.

"Lee is stuck to your front door handle, and he's on fire."

They approached Lee, who now had tears flowing down his cheeks. Marizama stroked him on his left shoulder three times. His hands separated from the scorching handle, and black smoke began shooting from his palms. He cried from the excruciating pain and then collapsed. After a couple of seconds, his hands became swollen and red.

Marizama gently rubbed her palms on his. Suddenly, his hands cooled down, and the pain disappeared.

"This magician stuff is hard for Lee. I don't think he likes it too much," Michael told her as she continued to rub Lee's hands.

"It doesn't come easy to him." Marizama brought his hands near her mouth and mumbled a chant as Lee awoke.

"How are your hands now?"

Lee lifted up his hands to look. "Cured, I think. Thanks."

"Thank you, Marizama," Michael added.

"Please inform me any time you're going out, because I always set my alarm for unwanted intruders. You could have burned to dust if I wasn't here, because nobody has the power to remove you from that door but me."

"We didn't know that," Michael said.

"I'm going to take a bath and change." Marizama went back into her bedroom.

Michael and Lee went back and sat quietly in the living room.

"Remember what I told you when we first met, that I only like to watch magicians. I don't think I'm cut out for this stuff. But you're not bad at it." Lee touched Michael's shoulder.

"I have to be good," Michael said.

"Why?"

"If I want to be the next King of Livingstone, I have to prove I can be a magician."

"Got it. Glad I'm not a prince."

"Not as easy as you thought, huh?"

"Not quite."

"Right now, I just want to get back to Livingstone and see what's happening with my family."

"Maybe Marizama can help you find another route to Livingstone. I want to go back to Thorn Valley. I think my friends are probably looking for me."

Marizama called them into the kitchen. After getting bathed and changed, she had prepared egg salad and tuna fish salad sandwiches.

"You're quite a magician," Michael told her.

"My magic isn't as strong as yours. I only have a little to protect myself."

"Whenever I see you, I always think there's something deeper about you," Michael said, taking a bite of his sandwich.

"Lots of people tell me that."

"Do you still want to walk around the neighborhood?" Lee asked once they finished their food.

"Yes," Michael answered.

"Do you want me to come with you?" Marizama asked.

"If you want to," Michael answered.

"All right; let's go," she said, straightening her flowered chiffon dress.

"You look so glamorous today," Michael told her.

"Thank you, Michael." She passed in front, and they followed. Scared to touch the door, they waited for Marizama to lead. She stopped, stared at them, and gently smiled before opening the door.

"Are you just leaving your door open like that, without locking it?" Lee asked.

"It appears unlocked, but no unwanted intruders will enter unless they are permitted."

"So, where are you taking us today?" Lee asked.

"I have no idea because I don't know what you boys want to see. You'll have to give me a clue I can work with." A gentle breeze feathered their hair as they walked.

"Marizama, would you be able to survive in my kingdom?" Lee asked her.

"I can survive anywhere, trust me. I have been to the four corners of the earth, but I prefer it here."

"Then maybe you can visit us in Flomoville. I'll be delighted to show you around. It's nicely organized. I'll also show you the largest magic universities in our kingdom."

"That's very kind of you, Lee. I would be happy to come see where you live someday."

"What about my kingdom?" Michael asked.

"When I was there, I saw lots of wars. Women were house slaves. It was too violent for me, coming from this quiet and peaceful part of the world. Since then, I've never returned."

"How long ago are we talking about?" Michael asked.

"About three hundred years."

"I don't even know the names of any of my relatives who existed during that period. That's a very long time ago," Lee told Michael.

"I know," he agreed, wondering about Marizama. *Did she ever change? Or did she believe that life always remained the same?* he thought. Michael looked at her curiously, wondering if she was human, ghost, or animal.

"Do you know another route to Livingstone?" Lee asked.

"I know another way, but I think we should wait for Joan and her sister. This isn't something you boys should rush into alone. If you study my life, you will understand that I'm a patient person. I believe in helping people. There are lots of superheroes in this city, but they are usually quiet about it."

The warm sun glistened on their faces but seemed cool in comparison to the scorching heat on the gold mountain. There was something supernatural about this place, Michael thought. You could almost hear the tranquility in the wind. Michael wondered how long Azamerie had controlled the region.

"How do people in this city calculate the dates, months, and years?" Michael asked.

"What do you mean?"

"For example, let's say today is Sunday, and the month is March, and the year is 1901. How would you translate this into a Texdulonicram date?"

Marizama looked at Michael. "That's a smart question. This city has its own modern technological calendar system for detecting the different seasons. Unfortunately, we only have four seasons. We're three hundred years ahead of you, so I will leave you to do the math. They usually sell calendars in the central shopping plaza close to the Underworld Hotel."

"So how long do you think Azamerie has ruled Texdulonicram?"

"Nobody knows for sure. I heard that she ruled for many years with both men and women."

"What caused the men to rise against her?"

"They wanted to change the rules and make Texdulonicram more like Livingstone, but she refused. She wanted this place to be small and simple to rule."

"I see," said Michael, scratching his temple. "I think we should get back before the sisters come searching for us."

"Do not worry about them; I think I already told you that they will find us easily when they arrive," Marizama said.

"Yes, of course," Michael said. They continued to walk past the homes, some that appeared to be auditoriums, until they came to a tall, silver building.

"Can we look inside? Maybe we can get a cool drink. I am starting to get hot," Lee said.

"I don't think that's a good idea."

"Why?" Michael asked.

"Because if you enter that building, you will never come out, no matter how strong you are. Actually, the only person who ever came out of this building is Azamerie."

"How come? Have you ever tried entering it before?" Lee asked.

"No. The people who enter this building are usually lawbreakers. They run inside for protection, and nobody follows them. Then they find out they can't get out. It's a magical building with a lot of curses."

"It's a shame to have such a beautiful building in the city and not be able to enter it." Michael stared at the panes that reflected silver light.

"Well, you can now do something about it, being that the woman is dead. I think she used it as a hideout. But if you can make this building livable, I think the entire city would enter it, including me, to see what makes it so special."

"I'll pass. I have other goals right now, and I don't want to take any risks," Michael said.

After strolling around the neighborhood, they returned to the house. Michael and Lee dozed off in the living room, and Marizama rested in her bedroom.

Michael shifted restlessly on the chair. He tried to turn over, when he suddenly saw Joan sitting on the armrest staring at him. He let out a yelp.

"It's you!" Michael caught his breath. "How was your trip? And where is your sister?"

"It was great, and my sister is in the shower, cleaning up."

Lee heard them speak and woke up. "Welcome!" he said with a grin.

"Thank you." Joan smiled back at him.

"Have you seen Marizama yet?" Lee asked.

"As a matter of fact, we were with her before she went into her room to take a nap." Azashema came into the living room with her face beaming. Lee rose and motioned Michael toward the corner of the room.

"Have you noticed something yet?" he whispered.

"What?" Michael asked.

"They look very different now. Their complexions and bodies have transmogrified; they're so gorgeous."

Michael gazed at them and said, "I noticed that the first time I saw Joan's face."

"Okay, everyone come closer. We need to have a team talk," Joan called out. They gathered around each other.

"We missed you," Michael said, smiling carefully.

"Thank you, but we actually didn't miss you boys at all," Joan said sarcastically. The boys' faces dropped, and she quickly added, "Come on! I was just playing. We missed you too. That's why we wrapped things up pretty quick." They laughed together.

"Now, we have to see Patrick and the other Vasferes. There is something we can do to transform them into human beings. They have to pass a magical test with Straights Condition."

"What condition?" Michael asked.

"Well, my friend, we can't tell you what it is until we're standing face to face with them."

"Do you want Marizama to come with us this time?" Lee asked with a skeptical look.

"I don't think that's a good idea. We need a backup here, and Marizama is the perfect person. We must hurry before it gets late. We also have a meeting with the city this evening, remember?" Azashema reminded them.

"Do you think we'll make it on time, or should we just leave it for tomorrow?" Lee asked, showing his frightened side. Michael glared at him, and he straightened his back.

"It was your idea to help those Vasferes. If you think it isn't important, then we could trash it. As for us, we keep our word," Joan told them.

"Wait. I'll call Marizama and hear her opinion." As Michael was about to go toward her door, he saw her approaching.

"Oh. I was just coming to call you!"

"I know," she said, passing by him on her way to the others. "I heard everything, and I would say it's important to go and save those people. The city can wait until tomorrow. The women will be overjoyed if their husbands come back home. I'm not sure how long it's been since they've seen each other. Most of the women remember the period when there were men in Texdulonicram." Marizama looked at them one by one. "I'll stay here and watch out for you."

"Thank you so much. That's what we wanted to hear. So, let's go," Michael said, looking at Lee, whose mouth puckered into a fearful gaze.

"But we have a problem. The only way you can reach those Vasferes is by going through the gold desert, and it's completely covered with hot, melted gold, which could burn right through your bones," Marizama said.

"What are you talking about? We'll just climb the ladder," Michael suggested.

"Look here, and see what I'm talking about." She put her right thumb in her mouth and slapped the floor with her left palm. The floor turned into a television screen, and the entire mountain appeared. In the picture, they noticed that the ladders were gone and that the entire area around the mountain appeared just as she had said.

Marizama stared at Michael and Lee.

"How about coming back?" Michael asked.

"Unfortunately, that's the only way, but who knows? Things may change when you're there."

"Let's go and see what happens," Michael said bravely.

They got up, kissed Marizama on the cheek one at a time, and walked outside. Lee followed Michael, who walked with his shoulders held high like the group leader. The girls walked behind.

Michael was beginning to enjoy being a leader. Wasn't that what Professor Wandom wanted him to learn while at Thorn Valley? If he could get back to Livingstone, he would have a long talk with him.

At the site of the mountain, they felt the unbearable heat from across the street where they were standing. Michael asked them to walk ahead. They did. He stood at the curb faintly calling, "Frank! Frank! Frank! We need help. Quick!" But Frank didn't appear.

He was there for almost twenty minutes calling Frank's name, and then he saw the others walk back toward him.

"What on earth happened to you?" Azashema asked. "Are you all right? Tell us. Maybe we can help," Azashema said.

"Not really. There's nothing we can do at this moment," he said, looking into the distance.

The girls stared at each other, and then they looked at him. "What?" asked Azashema.

"Nothing, let's just go," Michael said. They crossed the street and entered the cave. They trekked along the path that led to the melted gold.

"We are friends, right?" Michael asked.

"Yes," Azashema answered, looking at Michael in admiration.

Just then, Joan came toward her. "Azashema, Michael, cut the emotions. It's not good for the magic," she said.

"It's just that we have to look out for each other as we have always done," Michael said. Then he turned to the girls. "If anything happens to me, you must travel to the land of Livingstone. Tell anybody you meet, and they will relay the message to my parents. If anything happens to Lee ..."

"Leave me out of this," Lee said sternly as he turned away from them.

"Come, all of you, and have a seat here! There's something I believe is missing here," Joan said. Michael and the girls sat together on the ground. The girls' eyes were glued on Michael.

"What's happening with you? You don't look the same since we got here. Friends share secrets. This job can only be done with trust, faith, and open communication, and that isn't happening here," Azashema said.

"You're right. I have been hiding a lot of secrets from you. But where is Lee?" he asked.

"Lee, are you there?"

Lee came running, looking excited. "We're rescued; Frank is over there waiting for you."

"Who's Frank?" Azashema asked.

Michael rose. "I'll be right back." Smiling widely, he left in a hurry.

"I had some serious business in Richtown to take care of," Frank explained. "I'm glad you're safe and that you managed without me. You are really learning to be a leader, Michael. About going through that melted gold in the cave, don't worry—just do what you know. I'll cover the rest for you and Lee. I already spoke with him, and he knows what to do.

"It's important for the girls to understand that you are great magicians. You're right to have doubt, but as I told you a long time ago, I'll always be with you. Anyway, I'll let you go because your friends are waiting. I want you to smile when you approach them," Frank said.

"Thank you so much. I'll see you around." Michael smiled at the human head that bobbed in front of him.

"For sure," Frank answered and laughed.

Michael went back and asked everyone to follow him, but Joan said they weren't finished with their discussions yet. Joan was the tough one, Michael thought, always looking out for her sister and trying to control the situation. She was probably the better magician, too.

"Don't worry; I was just joking with you." Michael said.

River of Gold

"**M**ichael, if we don't finish this discussion, we won't take a step away from here! We'll call it quits!" Michael knew why he liked Azashema better. She was gentler, more accommodating.

At this, Michael sat and carefully looked at them with a wide smile on his face as Frank had told him, but Joan kept a frown on her face.

"You girls are so pretty," he said, but Joan cut him short.

"You have already told us this so many times, and we are sick and tired of hearing it."

"I was just wondering if you knew how grateful I am to you girls for being so kind to us."

She cut him off again. "You've already told us that, too. Get up, and let's go do what we came here to do."

"Who's Frank?" Joan asked, not dropping the topic.

"Just a friend," Michael replied.

"What was he doing here?"

"Just visiting for a moment or two."

"I don't believe you."

"It's true."

"Joan, we're wasting time. Let's just get going. Let's find Patrick so we can get home on time and get some rest." Azashema came to the rescue, and Michael looked at her approvingly. With a smile, he gave them each a hand and pulled them to their feet.

Lee stood, grinning, without saying a word. Joan got up, glared at him, and shook her head.

"Now, we'll follow closely, and I don't want you to worry about us, because we'll be just fine. When we reach our destination, you should leave the talking to us," Joan told them.

"That's fine with us."

Michael turned to Lee. "Walk side by side with me, and be fast this time!"

When they got closer to the edge of the melted gold, fire was popping off it and dispersing into flames like firecrackers.

"What are you waiting for?" Joan asked.

"Let's move," Michael said.

As they took their first steps through the river of hot melted gold, their feet felt as comfortable as if they were walking in luke-warm water. Michael's large stride splashed in the gold as if he were in a pool. "This is nice, isn't it?"

"Naw! Get me out of here," Lee said, trying to get out of the liquid as fast as he could.

After an hour, Michael reached the gold mountain and saw the others waiting ahead for him. When the girls saw him, they covered their faces. Michael wondered why. When he looked down at himself, he realized he was completely naked. His clothes had been burned to ashes. That was strange. The gold didn't feel hot, but nothing about the Kingdom of Texdulonicram made any sense. *Azamerie adjusted it to her liking*, Michael thought, *against all the laws of nature* waited anxiously to see what would happen

"Why are you hiding from me? You should've hid from him first!" Michael pointed at Lee who realized that he, too, was naked. They ran behind a bush. At that moment, they heard their names being whistled from behind the little bush, and they knew it was Frank.

"Quickly! Take these clothes and put them on." He handed them two pairs of black trousers and gray shirts.

"Being friends with a prince has its benefits," Lee chuckled, and Michael poked him in the arm.

They got dressed quickly, thanked Frank, and then they walked back to the girls.

"You guys look handsome in those clothes. Like twins. Where did you get them?" Joan asked.

"Well, you know we're magicians. Let's get back to business," Michael said.

They entered the big, empty room with the thick gold walls.

"I think this is where we were. Do you remember what you did the last time before the wall door opened?" Michael asked Joan.

"I don't think it was me. You're mistaking me for Lee."

Michael stared at Lee, who passed by them without speaking and then started touching the wall everywhere his hands could reach. The wall didn't open.

"Are you sure we are in the right place?" he asked.

Michael turned to the girls. "What do you think?"

The girls wandered around the room to see if they could recognize anything.

"I think we're in the wrong place," Azashema said.

"Well, in that case, we have to search for the right place." Michael led them up a set of steps. They walked up to the top, turned left, and entered a large, bright room with light flashing in all directions from the shiny gold walls.

"I think we're here," Lee said. He walked past them and started touching the wall. Soon, they were all touching the walls everywhere. Suddenly, they all found themselves in a room so dark they weren't able to see each other.

"Michael, are you there?" Lee called out.

They quickly followed each other's voices until they assembled together and held each other's hands.

"I know we can't see anything now, but if we stay like this for a little while, we might be able to see a little more when our eyes become adjusted to the dark," Michael said.

After thirty minutes, they saw a big, bright light in the shape of a star swiftly cross their vision and disappear. For the next fifteen minutes, the entire room turned so bright that they were unable to see anything. They waited anxiously to see what would happen.

"Grrrrrrr." A Vasfere charged at them. As it came closer, Michael realized that a solid glass wall had been constructed around him and his friends. *Thanks, Frank*, he said to himself. Although he wanted to help Patrick and get some normalcy back to Texdulonicram, he knew it wouldn't be easy. They heard several more growls and barks as the Vasferes lined the wall, their wide, long teeth ready to tear at them.

"Patrick! Patrick!" Michael bellowed, hoping that their leader would hear in the midst of the fierce growling. He walked farther back against the glass pane and commanded more light into the room. In no time, there were torches hanging in every corner, and they saw the giant Vasferes angrily growling at them like dogs.

"I think someone should talk to these animals so they will understand it's us," Lee suggested.

"You're right." Michael took a step forward and said, "We hope you recognize us because we were here some time ago, and we promised Patrick we'd be back."

"Are you the people who want to make us human again?" one of the giant, hairy Vasferes asked, approaching the pane.

"Exactly. That's why we're here. Please let us speak to Patrick."

A Vasfere approached, glared at them, and smelled Lee's feet under the glass pane. He announced, "Yes, I know them! They are here to make us humans again." The other Vasferes in the room moved back as the glass pane vanished. The Vasferes now bantered happily among themselves.

"Patrick is at his residence. I'll go call him," a Vasfere said to them. "I am Natamilxom."

"Nice to meet you." Michael shook his claw.

"Patrick's house is a bit far from here. Why don't you follow me?"

"Sure," Michael said, walking behind him.

Natamilxom trotted quickly ahead, wanting them to walk faster. After they had walked halfway to Patrick's house, he stopped and turned to them. "Why do you want to help us?"

"No one should suffer like you," Azashema answered.

"Who are these women?" Natamilxom asked.

"Our partners," Michael answered. "Look, we know you are great men who can bring prosperity and normalcy to Texdulonicram. Now that Azamerie is no longer, we have to find a way to return this kingdom to what it was before she arrived. You creatures have been living together all these years in total peace and harmony."

"Do you know why? It's because we don't eat or drink," Natamilxom answered as they reached Patrick's house. "Wait here."

Natamilxom entered a cave on the other side of the gold mountain.

"I'll be very happy to see how they look in human form," Michael said.

"Me too. I hope they'll cooperate and work with us to make their dreams a reality," Joan said.

"By the way, we appreciate how you talked to these Vasferes. Nobody got hurt, which is important," Lee told Michael.

"It's called leadership skills. They'll come in handy when I become king."

After a while, they saw Patrick barking furiously at Natamilxom, who had awakened him.

"I hope they develop human personalities after we change them," Azashema said.

As Patrick yelled at his Vasferes, he saw Michael and his friends watching him. He stopped and walked up to them.

"You actually came back as you promised. I never would have believed it. It's almost too good to be true. After all these years, we're going to be human again?" Patrick said happily.

"I think the time has come for you and your men to be set free as human beings. We will be pleased to help make your dreams a reality, but only if you and your men do as we command," Michael told him.

Patrick threw his head back in laughter. "No problem. Your wish is our command."

They walked back to the other side of the mountain, where the Vasferes gathered in anticipation. Some were singing and jumping around at the same time as they barked and growled like dogs.

Azashema and Lee watched as their eyes moistened with tears. Joan became bored and cut them short with, "Let's get this over with."

"Listen, she's right! You can wait here while I brief them on our conversation. I'll make sure they listen to your orders," Patrick said.

"There is much voodoo we must complete. Doing this will require a lot of sacrifices and courage from you. There are formulas which must be completed, and you must cooperate," Joan told him.

"You know what? We're prepared to do anything. Can't you see how delighted we are? Nobody has ever cared about us, and nobody has ever come here to see us but you," Patrick said.

"Do you have any assistants, maybe someone that you trust more than most?" Joan asked.

"Oh, yes. There are two of them."

"Then call them."

Patrick did, and they came forward. "My name is Dogpensen, and his name is Dogsen." They sat close to Patrick.

"Do you know how many of you live here?" Michael asked.

"We're 358,694 all together," Dogsen answered.

"And you said all of you are men?" Michael asked.

"That's correct," Patrick answered.

"We've tried to find the easiest way to help you. Our magic professors did all they could to discover a formula for your problems, but they were able to come to only one conclusion, which I think will be fine with you. My last question is: how come some of you have become so huge?" Azashema asked.

"That's simple. In the human world, everyone isn't equal. Some are short, and some are tall. Some are fat, and some are thin. It's the same in the animal world. How do you feel when you're talking to animals like us?" Patrick asked.

"I don't consider you animals; I consider you as one of us," Joan answered.

"Anyway, there's one task we must complete to get you out of here. First, you will be transmogrified into a female red deer and sent out to bring me the head of a famished female lion," she said.

The Vasferes glanced at each other in shock and asked her to repeat what she had just said. She did.

"This doesn't make sense at all. Can't you see how impossible this is? For the record, we don't have the power to transform ourselves into anything," Patrick said.

"You shouldn't worry about that. Remember, courage is very important in this situation," she reminded them.

"Okay. I hear you. Why don't we do as you want?" Patrick suggested, looking at Dogsen and Dogpensen, who both nodded in agreement.

"As I said earlier, you must do exactly as I tell you. It's your choice. If you are ready, we can start the procedure right away. If not, we're only wasting our precious time," she said.

"Okay. You're here to help us, and we know that," Patrick said. "Another thing: we don't have the power to pass through that door out there."

"Don't worry about that either."

Patrick stared at her suspiciously for a moment and asked, "Are you really here to help us, or have you come to complete Azamerie's job?"

Joan became angry, and Michael touched her arm to calm her. She stared back at Patrick. "We're here to help you."

"All right. Please give us a couple of minutes so we can talk this over."

The Vasferes moved away. They spoke one at a time in strange dialect.

"You guys were just standing there without helping me out," Joan complained to Michael and Lee.

"You told us earlier that we should leave the talking to you. You really spoke to them like a leader," Michael said. "As smart as Patrick is, he will read between the lines and come up with concrete conclusions."

Patrick and the others were trying to figure out if Michael and his friends were for real because their demands were so off-the-wall. After much consideration, Dogsen suggested that it was better to take the risk. After a few minutes, Patrick and the others came back to them.

"We agree to take the risk. It's better to die trying than to stay here forever," Patrick said.

"We will present you with the opportunity to assemble your men for a final discussion so we can get started," she said.

"We must make sacrifices if we want to get out there," Patrick said and quickly sent Dogpensen to assemble the Vasferes.

The Mysterious Savior

P atrick gathered twenty Vasferes for the mission. "We're all ready," Patrick said.

"Why did it take you so long?" Joan asked.

"Final preparations. I'm only trying to protect them, in case anything goes wrong," Patrick replied.

"So you're sending these ones first, right?" Joan asked.

"Do you want more?" Patrick asked anxiously.

"It's not that I want more; I'm only making sure."

She took out a small brown stick from her front right pocket.

"What is that?" Patrick asked.

"A Yougomore," Joan replied, lifting it up and down and watching it change colors from brown to blue.

"What does it do?"

"You'll see," Joan said. Then she asked Patrick to give the Vasferes his last words.

"There's nothing more to tell them. They know what their chances of surviving are."

"All right, push close to us." They did so with great anxiety.

Joan pointed her Yougomore at the Vasferes, and they immediately transformed into red deer and vanished. Joan moved back and slapped the floor. It changed into a big screen, so they could watch the deer.

Joan had sent them directly into a heavily treed forest where a large, famished female lion stood looking from side to side. She had been told that the lion had traveled all around the area for two days without food.

The deer moved about the woods where the trees shaded the rays of the sun. The lion heard the noise and slowly moved closer to investigate.

"They're in danger," Patrick said.

"Stay calm. This is all part of the procedure," Joan said.

The lion moved closer to the group of deer. She surveyed the deer and tilted her head toward the one she wanted to attack.

"She's going after Dogsen. He's my loyal servant," Patrick said.

"Be patient, Patrick. Joan is a great magician. I am sure she knows what she is doing. Look! It's going toward another deer," Michael said, and Patrick was relieved.

The lion moved in on the deer and vaulted onto the neck of one of them with its strong, long claws, butchering it instantly. All the other deer scattered in different directions.

Having been ravenous for so long, the lion didn't waste time. She ate the deer quickly. When she had finished, she turned to look around her and went searching for more. She leaped on one deer hiding behind a maple tree, but the deer fled. She licked the blood off her lips as she chased the deer for a couple of minutes before pouncing on it. They both collapsed to the ground, and she clutched it by the neck and killed it.

After eating, the lion went to rest under the deciduous tree. Her lids slowly shut, and she fell asleep in the shade. In the middle of her sleep, a wind blew ferociously, moving the branches of the trees from side to side.

"What's going on?" Patrick asked. "And where are my Vasferes?"

"Looks like they ran away," Azashema said.

"So, they failed the procedure?"

Michael was watching the screen; he didn't notice that Joan wasn't there anymore.

"I'm not sure," Michael said, turning to look at Joan, who had vanished. "Where did she go?"

"Who?" Lee asked.

"Joan."

"I don't know."

The wind hissed and blew branches off the trees. Suddenly, one of the dried branches of the deciduous tree broke off, and it pierced the lion's belly. The lion rose suddenly and tried to remove it, but it was too heavy. She was bleeding profusely and crying loudly; her penetrating voice scattered the forest animals as they ran for cover.

Joan suddenly reappeared in front of them with the lion's head. Michael turned to look at her and then did a double take. Lee, Azashema, and Patrick stopped watching the screen and turned to look at her.

"The lion's head is here!" Patrick yelled out.

"How on earth did you get it?" Lee asked.

She explained that she went into the forest as the lion was dying and cut off its head with a large knife.

"How come we didn't see you on the screen?" Lee asked.

"Okay. Watch carefully again."

She replayed the action. This time, they saw how it all happened. Patrick laughed out loud, jumping and dancing for joy. "Wait! How can we get the rest of the deer back?" he asked.

"They won't return until we are completely done."

The Vasferes sang and danced with Patrick.

"There's one more thing," she told Patrick.

"Please don't tell me to send more men. We're too happy now." His smiling face looked at her pleadingly.

She smiled back. "You will become humans again!" she shouted joyfully, dancing excitedly with Patrick.

"Joan, get back to work," Michael called out firmly. "No time to party yet. Finish what you started."

"I know, you want this over with so you can get back to Livingstone," she said.

"Yeah. I wouldn't mind going back. And did you forget about the town meeting? Finish it up."

Joan and her sister asked the Vasferes to gather in one space, and they did.

"Your friends have sacrificed their lives for you. Now go and stand with them and ask them to be still. It will take a while to prepare this head, but please don't move from your position. Whoever moves will never become human. Do you all understand me?"

They nodded their heads and started barking again. She asked Azashema to help clean out the lion's head. Patrick and the Vasferes stood still. They watched the girls with a trusting gaze.

"What is the meaning behind this head?" Lee asked.

"It's complicated and difficult to understand, but since you want to know, I'll tell you.

"The lion head signifies power, patience, determination, courage, and speed. We will give it to our god as a sacrifice. Then Azashema and I will gain the power to perform the ritual. It may look simple, but it's hard work. If something goes wrong with this sacrifice, we will both be exterminated. We're putting our lives on the line to save the Vasferes, but we know it's worth it," she said.

"As my sister has said, we are willing to do so to allow the Kingdom of Texdulonicram to return to what it was before Azamerie changed its rules," Azashema added.

"I don't get it. Are you telling us this because you think something might go wrong with this sacrifice?" Michael asked worriedly.

"We don't want to think negatively at this point. We want to go ahead now with the ritual," Azashema told Michael.

"Look, I kind of had long-term goals for you, Azashema," Michael said, looking at the ground.

"What do you mean?" she asked.

"Well, I thought that you might want to be the Queen of Livingstone one day."

"Michael, stop!" Azashema said, turning crimson.

"Michael, let us get back to work. Didn't you say you wanted us to complete the procedure?" Joan asked.

"Yes, but I didn't think it might cost you your lives," he said, looking at Azashema.

"Michael, my friend, our lives are at stake," Patrick called out.

"During the sacrifice, if you see us disappearing, you must use your magic power to catch us. If you see us surrounded by water, you must pull us from it. Only great magicians like you and Lee can do this," Joan said. "Our lives will be in your hands."

"Don't worry about a thing. Nothing bad will happen to you as long as we are standing here watching. Go ahead with the sacrifice, and leave the rest to us," Lee promised with a grin, becoming suddenly confident. But Michael wasn't so sure. Suddenly the stakes were too high, he thought.

The girls bent over the lion's head and started speaking in a strange dialect. They chanted and chanted, and their voices echoed around the room.

"I think they are speaking in their native tongue," Lee said.

Michael cut him off. "We'll talk about this later when they are done. We don't want to endanger them in any way."

After some time, they saw thick blue smoke firing from both Azashema and Joan's heads and noses. They were elevated four feet off the floor above the lion's head. After a few seconds, they saw an elderly man with a long white beard and an elderly woman with white hair, both dressed in long white robes. Michael and Lee couldn't understand the instructions they presented to the girls, but they could hear them murmuring.

As the old couple spoke, they took heaps of the blue smoke and rubbed it around their bodies. This went on for several minutes before the old couple disappeared.

Azashema and her sister slowly descended to the ground as the smoke started to clear up little by little. The lion's head had vanished, and they were both holding longer Yougomores than the one Joan had before.

After they stood quietly for about a minute, white ropes appeared and bound them together like bandages from their feet to their heads. Soon after, a red liquid, like blood, started flowing down from their heads onto the rest of their bodies; they were completely soaked and covered with the liquid. After several more minutes, the liquid disappeared and the white rope started to loosen from around their bodies. Then it vanished. The girls finally came back to themselves and walked over to Michael and Lee, smiling.

"That was one of the greatest magic procedures I have ever seen. You girls are so powerful," Michael said. He was now planning to continue talking to Azashema about being his fiancée, because each time she smiled at him, he lost his balance and became overjoyed.

"Don't ever overlook the powers of a woman. Now, let's go and get the party started," Joan said.

"I just want you to know we're still here ready to help. You see, where we come from, men are responsible for all the heavy duties. We don't like to see our women looking all stressed out," Michael joked.

Azashema kissed Michael softly on the forehead and whispered in his ear, "We'll talk about this later." He held on to Lee just to make sure he wouldn't tip over.

"You know, I have been noticing something about you lately. I will tell you when this party is over," Lee told him.

"Come with me, boys!" Azashema called out.

They walked to where the nervous Vasferes were gathered. When Patrick saw them approaching, he shouted, "Stand up! Nobody move! Today will be a day to remember for the rest of your lives!"

"Michael, Lee, stand away from us!" Joan said.

They moved back quickly. The girls moved very close to the group, one at the far right and the other at the far left. They took out their Yougomores and asked the Vasferes to be as quiet as they could.

The girls started chanting in their magic dialect, and their voices echoed back at them as they spoke. As the sound increased, the boys suddenly saw a bright light spread over the entire multitude of Vasferes. The room became dark for a few minutes, and then lit up again. Michael noticed that the girls weren't there; they had disappeared.

The Vasferes' bodies had transmogrified into humans, but their heads remained the same. Red and yellow light moved through them. Suddenly, the girls returned and stood in their former positions; their eyes appeared red, and their bodies were so bright, it was difficult to glance at them.

They started chanting again, and their voices became louder and louder with the echoes. After a few minutes, Michael saw a group of young men and women about his age covered head to foot in long black robes. They were patrolling among the Vasferes, touching their chests and whispering in their ears as the red and yellow light continued moving speedily among them.

After about two minutes, the room became so bright that no one was able to see through the light. It stayed on for two minutes before dying down. Azashema and her sister stood side by side, back to normal.

Michael and Lee suddenly saw multitudes of attractive older men and a few young men in their late teens standing and staring at them, but they appeared to be frozen. Michael and Lee heard Azashema and Joan call to them excitedly.

"They are calling us," Lee said.

"But they aren't finished yet."

"Let's see what they want," Lee said, walking toward the girls.

"We're having a little problem, and we need your help," Azashema said.

"What's the problem?" Michael asked.

"Well, we have done our job. Now we need you to complete it. As you can see, they are complete human beings now. They look like they did before they were transmogrified. We want you to bring them to full recovery so that they will be able to move, think, speak, and remember their past."

"That's easy. As I told you earlier, as a team we will make sure this job is successfully completed. Lee and I will take it from here," Michael told them. "Are you ready, Lee?"

"Whenever you are."

"Come with me." Michael turned and looked the girls straight in the eyes. "Are you sure you need our help, or do you just want to test our strength?" Michael asked suspiciously.

"We'll talk later when you are done," Azashema answered.

"All right. Stand clear and watch. You must be completely silent. If you speak out for any reason, or even if you laugh, you will become crazy or lose a great amount of your magical powers," Michael warned. The girls looked at him skeptically.

Michael walked among the men, planning what to do. He began to whisper Frank's name, and Lee heard him.

"Don't do that! He already told us what to do. He's around some-place watching, I am pretty sure," Lee whispered.

"Can you show me Patrick?" Michael asked.

"It's hard at this moment. Maybe he's that short guy in the front there," Lee answered, pointing to one of the Vasferes, who all looked like regular men now.

"Okay. Let's get to work quickly before it gets dark," Lee said.

"You go to the far left, close to that last man, and then stretch both your hands toward their chests, and I'll go to the far right and do the same," Michael said. They separated.

As soon as they stretched their hands, a red light shot out from their palms and toes, flying like a current through the multi-tude of men. Michael turned red as if he was on fire, while Lee remained normal; although, at that moment, neither of the boys was in his regular frame of mind.

The heat from the current was becoming unbearable by the minute. Red lights started flashing from above Michael and Lee's heads and entering the men's chests. Then, suddenly, all the lights disappeared. After a short while, Michael and Lee came to them-selves and glanced around.

"We're done. It will take just a few more minutes," Michael said. The girls sat on the floor, silent and exhausted. Michael and Lee sat with them, trying to convince them to say something.

"You boys did a great job. I know I shouldn't be telling you this until you finish, but I can feel your powers," Azashema told Michael.

"We wanted to complete the procedure ourselves, but we were just so tired. It almost makes us think we aren't good magicians," Joan said in frustration.

"No, don't say that. That's why we're a team. We're here to help. Sometimes it is impossible to do it all by yourself. We think you're great magicians, and we really respect you," Michael said.

"We made their dream a reality. Trust me," Lee said, pointing with his head to the men beside him. "Soon all those men will thank you. Then you'll realize what saviors you are."

Michael Isn't Believed

J oan and her sister still weren't persuaded, but they kept quiet, waiting to see what would happen next. They began to hear a group of men talking to each other, so Michael and the others ran to investigate.

To their surprise, they discovered the group strolling around in different directions as if confused. Azashema and her sister stood aside and watched in excitement as pools of tears collected in their eyes. Michael and Lee moved in to happily greet the men.

As he began speaking to them, Michael realized that there was a problem. The men didn't recognize Michael and his friends, nor could they remember who they were. While Michael and his friends started to introduce themselves, the entire group concluded that they had never seen them before.

Michael quickly ran to the front, stood on a rock, and called for attention. He started calling some of the names he knew: "Patrick! Dogpensen!" This drew their attention. The entire group was glaring at him, while two men scampered from the back to the front.

"I'm Patrick," said a young blond man. He rubbed his thick brown brows and looked at Michael with the same penetrating brown eyes he had had when he was a Vasfere.

"Michael." Michael thrust his right hand toward Patrick for a handshake, but Patrick didn't respond. "Me and my team, here, changed you back into humans."

"You're a liar. How did you know our names, and where are you kids from?" Patrick asked, but before Michael replied, he continued. "We were just invited by Azamerie for a conference to talk about augmenting our city."

"Do you even know where you are right now?" Michael asked.

"Yes, we're in the gold mountain, and we have been holding our meetings here for ages," Dogsen answered curtly. "We don't know what you kids are doing here. I think you should be in bed by now. By the way, who are your parents?" Dogpensen asked furiously. Some of the men angrily grabbed them and hurled them against the wall.

"I can't believe this," said Lee. "We've helped them so much, and all we get is a slap in the face. I knew these people wouldn't appreciate anything. I say we get out of here."

"I don't think that's a good idea. These men can only remember the first time they entered this room. I say we stay right here and use our powers to help them better understand what happened. What do you think?" Michael said to Lee and the girls.

Azashema and her sister whispered in each other's ears for a few moments.

"We've devoted a lot of time to this," Azashema began, "and I think we're going to stay and figure out how we can solve this problem."

Lee had no other choice but to stay with the others. Michael sat on the rock and Lee and the girls sat on the ground around him. The men suddenly started to march out of the door, looking dispirited. The man in front was about to penetrate the second door, when they saw bright lightning strike from the corner, hitting him on the stomach. He flew backward into the other men. With a large hole in his abdomen, the man died instantaneously. Some of the other men in front had minor burn marks around their faces and bodies.

"Don't panic, gentlemen," Patrick yelled out, lifting both his arms in the air. "We will quickly figure out why this happened. In the meantime, nobody goes through that door." They covered the dead man and dragged him farther inside.

"Maybe it's Azamerie who's trying to kill us!" roared one of the men, and the crowd rebuked him for the evil he had just spoken about their queen.

"Okay. I think this might have been a mistake. The first thing I want us to do is to take this man to his family for a good burial," Patrick said, standing near the covered corpse.

"If we wait here without telling them what is happening, they will all be killed. We are here to help them, so we had better get up now and do it," Michael said.

"You'll have to be patient, my friend. We must wait until it happens again before we move in," Joan told him.

"Why?"

"Because these men never seem to learn, and they won't listen to us."

"If we have to use our power to subdue them, we will," Azashema added.

"But if we don't act now, they'll kill themselves," Michael said, concerned.

Soon the men tried passing through the identical door for a second time. This time, two men in the front were hit on the head so heavily that their brains were scattered all over the others. The power from the current pushed the group of men backward and followed them into the room, burning almost all of them.

"Help! Get us out of here," screamed one of the men. "Help us before we faint!"

"Get some water!" screamed another.

"We want out!" a group chanted. "We want out!"

They pulled the two dead men to the side of the room and covered them.

"I told you not to go through that door," Patrick said forcefully. "Stay put if you want to stay alive."

"We'll try to find another way out of here," Dogpensen added, facing the crowd.

As the men were talking noisily, they noticed Michael and his friends again.

"What are you doing here? Thought we told you to leave us alone," Dogpensen said.

"We can get you out of here alive, but first, you must believe everything we told you earlier. If you don't, then we will let you stay here and die, because there's only one way out of this room—through that door," Michael said, pointing to the door through which they had entered.

"Yes, we know that! Now you get out of here because we don't need your help!" Patrick said rudely. This time, Michael and Lee had had enough. They started to walk away, but Azashema and her sister ran after them, begging them to stay.

"After all that has just happened, you still don't understand there's something deep going on here! You need to open your eyes right now before it's too late!" she said, looking frustrated.

Dogpensen came toward them, glaring at them from top to bottom. "When I count to three, I want to see you gone!" He counted to three, but the girls remained, frowning at him. "We don't know what you want, and we don't want to hear your silly stories anymore. Get out! Get out now!"

Dogpensen and some of the other men tried to force the girls out of the door that produced lightning, but they couldn't. The girls stood their ground firmly as the men began beating them; they didn't even notice that they didn't get a scratch on their bodies.

"All you stupid fools! We're sick and tired of your selfishness! We're about to take control of this our way!" Joan said furiously.

Patrick heard them and asked, "What did you just say?"

The girls repeated themselves.

Patrick walked back to the crowd shouting, "Kill them! Kill them!"

The group of men rushed at the girls, but they stood defiant, watching the men without blinking. Michael and Lee saw smoke coming from the girls' fingers, which was starting to spread through the entire room.

"What's going on here?" one of the men asked as he began coughing.

"Where is that smoke coming from?" Patrick asked.

"I can't see anything," Dogsen said.

The noise of the men quieted down as the dark haze dimmed the room further and further. Only Michael, Lee, and the girls could see clearly.

The men sat on the floor sulking; some were crying. After the smoke had cleared, Michael could clearly see some of the younger men banging on the floor with their hands, shaking their heads, and crying loudly. Michael and Lee walked around the room and asked them why they were crying.

They all had long and sad stories to tell, but the more Michael bent down to comfort them, the harder they cried. This was taking up a lot of time, and Michael and his friends were getting tired and wanted some rest.

Joan went to the front and yelled out, "That's enough! You will stop crying right now, or you will get a piece of me!"

They turned to look at her. The crying was reduced to whimpering, when Patrick came up to her and told her that his people were ready to accept her demands.

"Good! Then you go tell them to listen carefully. I'll tell you once again who you were and who you are now, and then I'll tell you what you must do to get out of this place alive!"

"Strong lady," Lee said admiringly.

Patrick did as Joan said, and the group became quiet and focused.

Joan took her time and explained everything, but they still refused to believe her.

"With all due respect, we would like you to prove what you're telling us because, frankly speaking, we think you're just making up this story to get us to do what you want," Patrick said.

"Why is it you're the only one speaking?" Lee asked.

"Because I'm their leader and, besides, it doesn't make sense for us to speak together," Patrick answered rudely, as the group laughed at Lee.

"Shut up! All of you, right now!" Joan angrily screamed as she turned to Lee. "You must be very hard on them, or they won't respect us!"

"I'm following your lead," said Lee.

Knowing that Frank was right there with him and ready to help, Michael moved to the front and asked Patrick to come closer, which he did. Michael took off his shirt and shined the wall clean. He put his shirt back on as his friends gathered to watch. He slapped the gold wall. Immediately, a big screen appeared. Patrick sat back and watched the men's lives from their final encounter with Azamerie, to their change into Vasferes, and to their change back into men.

After watching, Patrick went back and told his men that Michael was trying to hypnotize him into believing their depressing stories. He and his men started laughing at Michael and his friends.

At that moment, Michael heard his name called from the far corner. He told his friends he would be right back and walked toward the sound. He saw Frank bobbing up and down.

"Can you imagine this? After all we have done, it is as if we are still at zero. We are not getting anywhere."

"I think you're beating around the bush too much," Frank said.

"What do you mean?" Michael looked at the men intently from a distance.

"Just get back there and glare hard at them, like you're doing now, and leave the rest to me. They will take a nap and wake up not acting this way anymore. Trust me; they will believe everything you've told them."

"You won't transmogrify them back to animals, right?"

"No, I wouldn't do that. I think they were transformed into men in the wrong way. That's why you're having a problem. Now, you'd better go back. Your friends are waiting."

Michael went and asked his friends not to bother anymore, but Patrick came up to them and asked, "Where is Azamerie?"

"She is dead," Lee answered anxiously.

Patrick laughed madly. "How did you kill her?"

"I didn't tell you we killed her! It sounds funny to you right now, but if it were up to me, I would've walked away and left you to help yourselves. We have better things to do than sit here with a bunch of airheads, pretending to know it all. I see why Azamerie tried to kill you!" Lee said. Patrick lifted his hand to strike Lee when Joan pointed her finger, releasing smoke and momentarily blinding him. Lee gave Joan a grateful look.

Without speaking, Michael walked to the front and started glaring at the men. Lee and the girls were confused.

"What are you doing?" Lee asked.

"Leave it to me," Michael replied and continued glaring from side to side. After twenty seconds, the men passed out and fell down on the floor.

"Don't touch them!" Michael warned.

"What did you do to them?" Azashema asked.

"I just made them feel exhausted so they will take a little nap. When they wake up, we won't have to convince them anymore, and this mission will be terminated," Michael said with a grin.

"You see how aggravating this has been. I think we're the most sympathetic and patient people in the whole world, and I am glad to be part of this massive operation," Michael said.

"What happened?" When Michael looked up, he saw Patrick standing above him and questioning him.

"What do you mean?" Joan asked in response.

"It seems we were here for a meeting with Azamerie, but she didn't show up, and after a while, I saw Dogsen change into a Vasfere. When I glanced around, I suddenly saw nothing but animals barking at me, and when I looked at my hand, it was a dog's paw. I don't know what happened after that. Now I have just woken up, and I see you here."

"Now do you fully understand what we've been trying to tell you all day?" Michael asked.

"What were you telling us?" Patrick asked, looking surprised.

"Never mind," Michael said.

Patrick walked around, helping everyone stand up. After they all realized what had happened to them, there was nothing more for Michael and his friends to explain.

Patrick walked backed to the boys and girls. "It has all come back to us. I mean … we remember everything." He embraced Michael. "Thank you for helping us. We owe our lives to the four of you."

"Finally, we're communicating. It's wonderful!" Michael told his friends.

He turned back to Patrick and smiled. A long line of men pushed forward to thank Michael and his friends. Many of the men shook their hands, some embraced them; others offered to have them to dinner at their homes with their wives, if they could ever find a way to get out. Michael felt like a king. This reminded him of the royal parties his mother and father had held at the palace where kinship reigned.

"Okay, people, we don't have much time. In a couple of hours from now, it will be dark outside. We have to find a way to get you out of here alive," Michael said.

"What do you want us to do now? We don't want to lose any more men," Patrick said tensely.

"We want you to calm down. You should rejoice because everyone will walk through that door alive, so don't panic," Michael promised. He took his friends to the door into the other room. "As you all know, we have just one last problem."

"I think we should contact Marizama and know her views," Azashema suggested.

"But we don't have gold dust to contact her," Lee said.

"All we have to do is call her names five times and she will appear," Azashema said.

"All right then. What are we waiting for? Start calling her name," Michael said.

Through the Door

zashema called Marizama's name. After five times, her face appeared on the gold wall right above them.

"We are excited to see you again. Thanks for showing up," Michael said.

"I was waiting to hear from you all day, and I began to panic," she began. "I don't know why, but for a long time, I wasn't able to track you down. I already know some of the problems you're having, but first, I want you to tell me everything."

Azashema explained the problem they were facing.

"There's nothing I can do to help in your present situation." Marizama twirled the purple scarf around her neck between nervous fingers. "There's a big, invisible horse sitting right outside. It has a rope tied around its neck, and that rope is attached to the top and bottom of the door where the men tried to exit. It has a built-in sensor, which has a bit of every one of the men's blood in it. It also has mighty powers to directly convey lightning from the sky to that door, and it will strike and burn anybody whose blood is in its sensor.

"Now, the problem is this: I can't detect what kind of rope it is, and that horse isn't an ordinary horse. When in danger, it grows a horn in the middle of its forehead like a unicorn, and this gives it extra power to destroy anything that comes close to it.

"It has been sleeping for centuries, which is why you can stay close to it without getting hurt. I have being researching my magical database, but I couldn't detect a formula that will easily get those men out. I'm sorry."

"On which side of the door did you see the white horse?" Michael asked.

"It's lying right behind you on your right, and it looks very warlike and very mighty. Please, don't ever try to touch that rope. It's very dangerous. It will give you a disease that has no cure. I think you still have a hell of a job ahead of you," she said.

"So, what are you saying?" Michael said.

"I suggest that you sit together and discuss this before starting anything," Marizama advised.

"All right. Thank you very much," Michael said.

"You're welcome. Please call me if you have questions about anything, and I'll be glad to help." Marizama disappeared.

"Okay, we have come this far, so we must finish this project. Now, I want to know who among you is with me," Michael said.

Lee, Joan, and Azashema told him that they were in.

"We should sit here and do some thinking," Michael suggested.

"I don't think that's a good idea," Lee said.

"Why?"

"Because we already know the enemy is sitting right here. There might be a good possibility it will hear our plans. I suggest we go inside to conclude our discussion."

"He's right," Joan agreed.

Michael stood on the rock. "Listen up! We have a bigger problem than we expected," he announced. "Azamerie was cunningly smart. She installed a strong force sitting right at that door prepared to annihilate any one of the men who goes through it, as we have already seen."

"So what are we supposed to do in this situation?" Patrick asked.

"That's what we're still trying to figure out. Now, what I want you and your men to do is to stay calm and not panic. We're focused on this problem, and it will be resolved somehow," Michael said.

"Did you say *somehow*?" Patrick asked.

Michael paused for a moment with his finger across his lips. He then stared back at Patrick. "Yes, somehow."

"That means you're not sure if you may never find a way out."

"No. It just means that we have to do a lot of planning, and you have to bear with us," Michael said. Then he walked back to his friends.

Patrick turned to his men, and they quickly surrounded him, but he had no comforting words for them.

"I think the first thing we must do is to make sure everything at that door is visible. Then we can try to wreak havoc on it," Azashema suggested.

"If the horse wakes up while we're in the process, don't you think we could be badly affected? And if we're affected, who will help these men?" Michael asked.

"That's why we must take the risk; we have to know what we're dealing with. We know the horse is sleeping, and I don't think it will wake up right now. I think we can conquer anything outside that door," Michael said with confidence.

"Just as Marizama said, we should give ourselves a few minutes to quickly think this over since we are the only ones allowed to freely move in and out of this room, and I will ask the men to think along with us," Michael said and walked toward the men. They agreed to let Michael and Lee do the job. They further promised to offer suggestions, if they thought of any.

Lee softly whispered to Michael, "Do you think Frank is still around?"

"Yes, he is talking to me and telling me what to do. Now, just follow my lead," Michael said. He took off his shirt, tore a piece off, and then put it back on. Lee did the same. Michael took the piece of cloth from Lee and held them both up in his right hand, keeping his left hand wide open.

A green light suddenly flew from behind and circled them a couple of times before entering into the pieces of cloth Michael was holding. When he looked down at the pieces of cloth, they were mended into one piece of fabric, and their color had changed to green. At that moment, Lee heard a voice murmuring as if someone was speaking to Michael, but he didn't see anybody with him.

Michael then kneaded the cloth on his face and passed it to Lee; he did the same and wanted to give the cloth back, but Michael told him to pass it to the girls. They did the same and then gave it to back to Michael. As Michael attempted to take the cloth from Azashema, it suddenly disappeared. The group began to search for it everywhere but couldn't find it.

"What the heck happened?" Michael asked in frustration.

"Look," Lee said, pointing to Michael's shirt. When he looked down at his shirt, he saw the green cloth mended back to the spot from which he had originally torn it.

"Look down," Michael told Lee, who looked at his own shirt and saw that it had also turned back into its original state. They walked over to the girls, frustration written on their faces.

"We've failed to locate the invisible horse. We're not able to do this, so maybe you girls should try," Michael said.

All of a sudden, Joan held onto her sister's arm and showed her what she was seeing. Michael and Lee turned to look. The horse and the rope had become visible. The horse was truly huge with red eyebrows, and it was still asleep. The rope was thick and long, and they could see red liquid flowing through it, like blood running through a vein. It was a scary sight.

"Let's get out of here before it wakes up," Lee whispered fearfully.

"Don't be scared; this horse won't wake up now. It has been sleeping for centuries upon centuries, and I know it will sleep for many more to come," Azashema said, frightened, her fingers shaking.

"Come on, guys. Someone is trying to get to us," Lee said. As Michael and the girls came closer, he said, "I heard a voice like Marizama's, and a tiny white light flashed from this wall." Right away, Michael called her name five times, and then she appeared.

"Enter the room at once. Something very important has just come up, and I want to talk to you about it." They did so quickly. After Michael slapped the wall with his palm, Marizama appeared inside.

"Now that you have made the horse and the rope visible, there's a greater possibility that you will be killed, along with all the people you are trying to save.

"That horse has extraordinary powers to draw lightning and fire from the sky, and the power of that fire and lightning is five times stronger than a house's current. That rope out there by the door could suck all the blood out of all those men and use it to bring Azamerie to life. I can see that they are working on her right now for this curse."

"Azamerie? But we killed her!" Michael cried.

"Yes, you tried, but the apes are trying to reform her from her own blood, and when they are done, she will become more powerful than she has ever been. You have the opportunity to kill her right now. Besides, that horse will soon be waking up," Marizama warned.

"Where is she now? And how much time do we have remaining?" Lee asked.

"On the right side of the mountain toward the bushes, there's a house that contains a big egg about the size of a regular football. It contains all the power you will need to destroy that horse and that rope in order to set all of you free."

"Free? What are you talking about?" Joan asked her.

"You think you're free because you can go in and out of that room, but pretty soon, if you don't do what I'm asking, you will all be in the same situation.

"Now, when you go out of the second door, there's a narrow pathway leading to the outside. Stand right at the edge and look down; you will see a ladder. That ladder will take you down to the ground. When you get to the ground, facing the ladder, turn right, walk directly into the bushes, and you will see the house.

"But please, don't get me wrong. That egg is strongly protected, and you will need great powers to get it. You have two hours and thirty minutes left, so please hurry."

"Oh, my! That is a very short time," Lee said.

"Well, I'm sorry. There's actually nothing I can do about that. I'm telling you what I can see in my database. I wish I could change things to make it a little easier for you, but I can't. And if I were you, I would get started right away."

"Suppose we forget about all this helping stuff; could we walk away clean?" Lee asked.

"At this point in time, you have no choice but to complete the mission because you have made the horse and rope visible, and there is no other way out of this predicament. You must stop asking too many questions and do what you are supposed to do before Azamerie awakens and takes revenge."

The screen vanished, and Michael turned toward the men. "Listen up, everybody; we're at the point of no return. Our hands are tied, and we have a strong storm ahead of us. Please remember that nobody should ever try to pass through that door. It might destroy our efforts. We will be back shortly."

"We will be praying for you," Patrick said.

Michael left with his friends, and they walked vigilantly by the horse. As they watched it, they saw a little horn growing in the middle of its forehead. Without talking, they followed Marizama's directions until they saw the ladder.

"Who's going first?" Lee asked, staring at Michael.

"I'll go in front," Michael volunteered. He got on the ladder, and Lee and the girls followed him down.

"Try to remember where we are so we will be able to find this place when we return," Michael said.

"We won't forget," Azashema told him.

They continued following the directions Marizama gave them, made it to the road leading through the bushes, and trekked farther in until they saw a little opening with a small, wooden house sitting on top of the hill. They stopped to investigate.

The group heard a sound moving around them, but they weren't quick enough to see what it was. It was getting closer and closer. They ran to hide under the bushes, but it was too late. Michael turned his head to look behind him and saw his friends on the ground, fast asleep.

"Get up, Lee! Azashema! Joan! Stop fooling around!" He started poking them, but they wouldn't wake up. When he turned back, he looked up and saw a giant squirrel sitting on a tree branch right above him. The squirrel gazed at him, and he collapsed and fell asleep.

When Michael opened his eyes, he was in an old, wooden house surrounded by squirrels that appeared to be eating something. Michael quickly searched for his friends to make sure they were all right, but he saw that Lee wasn't among them.

"Where is Lee?" he asked the girls.

"Look! He is over there, and they are going to eat him alive!" Joan said.

Michael angrily ran toward the squirrels, screaming, "Leave him alone!"

When the squirrels saw Michael, they quickly jumped to their feet and stood right in front of him, prepared to attack. They were three feet tall with fat, round bodies. Michael stopped and glared at them. He knew they were prepared for a fight.

Michael tried to make the squirrels understand that he meant no harm. "All I want is my brother. I will just pass right here without touching any of you and take him, and we'll be out of here in no time." He spoke politely.

"I can't let you do that. No one comes into my house and tries to control me! I, Quientso, am the man around here. I will tell you what to do and what not to, period! Now, go back and sit with your friends before I change my mind and eat you instead," the little squirrel said in a rough, but squeaky, voice.

Michael stood there, frozen. "You can't talk. You're a squirrel."

"I can do anything I want!"

"I know you're hungry, but squirrels don't eat human beings," Michael said, trying to reason with them. "All right, I tell you what; I'll take my brother and bring you more than enough of any kind of nuts you want. You name it."

The squirrels laughed. "You really think we would eat human? We only did some work on his dirty hair. Go! Take him!" Lee was still asleep from the squirrels' spell when Michael pulled him away. Joan and Azashema got up to help, and they noticed that his hair had been neatly braided.

After a little while, Lee woke up, looking all around the room. "What's going on here?"

"I'll tell you later," Michael said to Lee. Then he turned to the squirrels. "Thank you. We will be leaving now."

"You won't leave unless I tell you to," Quientso said.

"We have to go, actually. We would like to sit here and talk, but we have some important obligations to take care of," Michael said politely. He turned to his friends and told them to follow. He took a step, and his friends took a step behind him. As he was about to take a second step, he felt as if something heavy was attached to his legs, and he couldn't move them. The same thing happened to his friends. They looked at each other in confusion and knew they were in trouble.

Michael turned white with anger. "Now, what do you want?" he screamed.

Quientso said, "I want you to sit there and shut up because we're about to show you what you think you know."

"Who are you?" Joan asked.

"Shut up, young lady!" Quientso yelled at her.

"Don't tell me to shut up! Nobody tells me to shut up!" she yelled back at Quientso.

"You don't know who you're messing with."

They began to threaten each other, approaching each other aggressively as if they were about to fight. Michael quickly separated them.

"Joan, they're just squirrels. Let's just get out of here," Michael said.

"Now, wait a minute. You're looking for trouble, young man. We're squirrels, but we can whip your buttocks. In fact, we should start right now."

At that moment, all the squirrels held their positions and grew bigger and fatter. They pumped their muscles and pushed their chests forward as they furiously approached them. Quientso commanded them to freeze, and they obeyed. Michael and his friends were gasping hard with their fists up, prepared to throw a punch, finally able to move again.

"Who are you?" Azashema asked calmly.

"Why do you want to know who we are?" Quientso asked.

"You must be somebody. I know for sure all of you aren't squirrels," she said.

At that moment, they transmogrified into their human forms, and Michael was surprised to see some familiar faces.

"What are you doing here?" Michael asked with a smile.

"Do you know them?" Azashema asked.

"Oh, yes! I know them all," Michael answered. He ran to hug them and thank them for coming to his rescue. Among them were Professor Barclay, Serina, Professor Wandom's wife, and her friend Tarrance. Back in Livingstone, Professor Wandom had told Michael that Serina and Tarrance would be his caretakers during his stay at Thorn Valley.

"I want you to get something straight," Professor Barclay said. "We didn't come here to support you or help you in any way. I only came to inform you that I didn't expect you to stay in this kingdom for so long. As you know, the longer you stay here ... well, time isn't waiting for you."

Michael tried to explain the problem. Professor Barclay cut him off and told him to stop because he already knew it all. "You can't be a savior. Do you know what you have gotten yourself into by trying to save the world? I'm telling you now to abandon this mission and let me take you back to camp where you belong."

"Back to Livingstone? Yes, I'd like that," Michael said, looking at Lee.

"Traitor," Joan said. "You want us to finish this mission alone? Cop-outs! Now we know who you really are, Michael and Lee!"

"Professor, I don't mean to be rude or anything, but I won't go anywhere before helping those men," Michael began, turning to look at Azashema. "Look at my friends; they are human beings, too. They have risked their lives just to help me, and now you want me to walk away from them just like that. I don't think I can do that." Azashema looked at him proudly.

"This mission is very dangerous, and you and your friends have a high chance of not surviving it," Professor Barclay warned.

"Sir, you can talk directly to Michael and leave us out of this," Joan said. "I have a bad feeling about you, anyway, and I think something isn't right here."

"I think you should shut up before you get on my nerves!" Professor Barclay told her.

"You should shut up too, because your advice is senseless! We have urgent business to take care of, so if you'll be kind enough to excuse us before you regret this," she warned him.

"Who do you think you're talking to, little girl? Watch your mouth before I make you shut it. See what we almost did to Lee? Well, you'll be next," Professor Barclay barked. "Besides, I'm not talking to you or any of your friends over there, only to Michael. Why are you being so rude when you don't even know who I am?"

"You could be the greatest magician from Pluto—I don't care!"

Michael was watching them without speaking. He worried that time was passing and they still had a lot of work to do to help Patrick and his men.

"Thank you all for coming, but we have to go now." Michael walked over to his friends and asked them to follow him. As soon as they got out of the house, they saw Professor Barclay and his group standing in front of them.

"Okay, let me be truthful. We are not the people you think we are." Professor Barclay and Michael's caretakers laughed and then transformed themselves into hideous creatures.

Michael Uncovers the Key

The people Michael thought were his friends were now hideous Boscrollis. Michael looked at the creatures, which loomed imposingly in their resemblance to large bulldogs, and panicked. About four feet tall and almost four hundred pounds each, with wings on both side of their back, the Boscrollis had taken to the air and were flying toward them. The four young ones fled, frightened, in all directions.

This is so unlike Professor Barclay, thought Michael, who had initially been welcomed by the professor to Thorn Valley. He saw their four long, white front teeth and their dangerously sharp claws shaped like the edge of an arrow. Michael began trembling. *What do they want? And where is Frank?* After the Boscrollis landed on the ground, the ground vibrated with the movement of their feet. There were over a hundred of them. Some, however, flapped their wings and flew away, leaving only a few.

As Lee and the girls started to quiver, Michael told them to be strong. He bravely approached the Boscrollis and said in a low voice, "We have seen Boscrollis like you before!"

One of the Boscrollis walked to the front, smelled at him menacingly, and screamed, "We're the real Boscrollis, and your mission will end here!" As it spoke, a flame popped out of its mouth and scared Michael with its strong heat.

The Boscrolli went back to the others and spoke with them. Michael asked in a loud voice, "Aren't you Professor Barclay?"

One of the Boscrollis turned and said, "I wish I was."

Then another one said, "We are planning how to separate your body parts and sacrifice you to our gods as an offering because you're young and fresh."

"Then what are you waiting for? Come and get me," Michael screamed at him.

"Don't rush, take it easy. We'll soon come to a conclusion, and then we'll be with you. I don't think it will take that long."

"How do you know Professor James Barclay?" Michael asked.

"We're great magicians, as you are, and some of us can see beyond what you humans see. While you were asleep, we opened your brain and found out what your mental capabilities and magical strengths are. We've analyzed them and realized we are powerful enough to exterminate you without a hassle. We now know more about you than you would ever surmise."

This unexpected revelation flooded Michael with fear.

"Where are you, Frank?" Michael begins to whisper. Nobody heard what he was saying, but Lee reminded him to stop and do what Frank had told him to do.

"We know why we are here," Michael began to his friends. "We have to get that egg. I suspect these Boscrollis are the ones protecting it. Now let me tell you a little about determination. It is the process of deciding what you want to do. We have the fortitude to help those thousands of men ensnared in that mountain and also to save our own lives. Are you with me?" Michael asked.

They put their hands together and said in unison, "Yes!"

The Boscrollis heard them and turned quickly. "We're ready." As they moved in for the kill, Michael and his friends stood in a circle holding hands, waiting for their magic power to regenerate.

"We shouldn't move or panic," Joan said. "I will tell you when to move."

Suddenly, the Boscrollis rushed at them with black smoke shooting from their mouths, eager to tear them apart. The black smoke penetrated the entire area as they sprang at Michael and his friends. But then, the creatures were forcibly stopped; it was as if they had smacked against a thick iron wall. The sound was metallic, as if they really did strike an iron barrier; it pinged and vibrated heavily in the Boscrollies' ear as they fell helplessly to the ground. Some of them broke their front teeth and cringed in pain as blood collected around their mouths.

Their eyes reddened, and becoming fiercely violent, they tried to force themselves through the thick glass wall Michael and his friends had magically built around themselves. The Boscrollis' claws scratched on the surface of the glass trying to break in.

"You miscalculated our powers," Michael yelled out brazenly. "Now we know you aren't magicians but a bunch of blood suckers!"

"Listen, you little rat! When I lay my hands on you, I'll tear you apart!" the Boscrolli that had changed from Professor Barclay said aggressively.

"We have decided to let you live, and I tell you that today is your lucky day!" Azashema said.

The Boscrolli began to strike other Boscrollis around him with its wings, screaming madly as it flew crazily up and down and flung dust from the earth below.

Thinking fast, Michael and Joan created a Domionatic, a magical flying machine which appear to look like a double sized telephone booth, out of the glass enclosure around them, so that they could all fly to find the egg as Marizama had instructed. He stood at its controls and looked outside through the four sides of the transparent flying machine. The sight infuriated the Boscrollis, who flapped their wings angrily, rising higher into the air. Michael headed toward the egg's location. It was quite a distance from where they were, and as they flew, the Boscrollis flew alongside them, striking their Domionatic with all their might in an effort to break the glass. Undeterred, Michael and his friends stood inside laughing and making jokes.

"Look at that one. His eyes look like they are in the back of his head!" Joan said and Lee laughed.

"Red as laser beams," Lee said with a wide grin, pointing with both hands at the Boscrollis.

The more the group mocked the Boscrollis, the more aggressively they hit the Domionatic. They began to fly speedily in groups. Each group continued to strike the machine, but it did not even shake.

The Domionatic flew all the way to a creek. The Boscrollis couldn't go across the creek because they knew that it was a powerful wizard's territory, so they turned and flew back in frustration. Michael flew the Domionatic across the creek and saw a little house in the woods on top of a hill, where Marizama had told them the egg would be.

"We can't go to where the egg is," Joan said.

"Why?" Michael asked.

"Because as a magician, I know the capability of this object I created," she answered.

They parked the Domionatic behind the house. As they came out onto a grassy stretch, Azashema sealed the aircraft magically.

"I'm hungry. Why don't we go in that house and see if there is something to eat," Lee suggested.

"Don't be naive. We're in an unknown territory. You can't just enter people's houses like that; you might get yourself killed, and I won't allow that to happen," Michael said, hearing the gurgle in his friend's stomach.

Lee held Michael's arm affectionately, then walked passed him and the girls and trekked ahead without looking back.

"Why isn't Lee walking with us?" Azashema asked Michael.

"I think all of this is just too much for him," Michael said. "Not everybody is cut out for this stuff. I mean, we came to learn magic at Thorn Valley, but I don't think he knew the magic we would have to perform would be this intense."

"I think he needs my protection," Joan said with a smile.

"Looks like you want to make him your project," Azashema said, winking at her sister.

"Look what Lee is doing," Michael said.

They came closer to him and saw three giant, ugly ape-women sitting ahead glaring at him.

"See, I told you. Without us, he gets into trouble every time," Joan said.

The apes were large and muscular, with long black hair dangling almost to the ground, and they sat with their mouths open, exposing their protruding black teeth. Lee looked to the right and then to the left. He saw the apes on both sides and began to retreat.

"He looks as if he saw something deadly. He's scared," Joan said.

They stopped and waited until Lee backed up to where they were. He began to murmur about what he had seen, but before he got through speaking, the group of apes surrounded them.

"I think you should try to talk to them," Azashema suggested to Lee.

Lee looked around and then turned to her. "Why is it always me?"

"What are you talking about?" she asked back, confused.

"Can't you see Lee's scared?" Joan said, protectively putting her arm around him.

"Scared? Me? No way. I'll prove it to you. Just watch," Lee said and turned toward the apes.

"Hello, apes," Lee said cautiously. He introduced himself and his friends. As he was talking, he decided to move a little closer. He attempted to take a step forward, when one of the apes lunged crazily in an effort to bite him, but Lee dodged the assault. Michael told him to stay firm in his position, and he complied. He quickly explained everything about their sudden visit, and the apes listened attentively.

"Nobody takes my egg. The next time the word egg is mentioned here again, I'll tear the person to pieces. Understand?" the biggest ape said with her saliva flying into Michael's face. "Do you know how long we've been working on it to bring it to this stage? Do you know how many lives we have lost for that egg? You're lucky to even be standing here in front of us alive."

"What's your name?" Joan asked.

"Why do you want my name?" she asked back.

"Because it is easier to address you by your name when we're talking about this important issue."

"My name is Momkey Weslorsdc. What are your names?"

She reintroduced them. "I thought you understood our name when Lee introduced us earlier."

"Wait a minute! Are you trying to call me dumb?"

"No! I would never call anybody dumb. Why would I want to use such a word on you? What evil have you done to me?" Their eyes moist, the apes turned away from them.

"Why are they crying?" Lee asked.

"I don't know. Maybe what I said hurt their feelings," Joan said.

"It isn't that," the ape said. "See, we were smart women in Texdulonicram. We each had high-paying jobs, husbands, and children. Azamerie became mad because we challenged her way of doing things. She changed us into apes." Tears poured down the apes' faces.

"That's awful," Azashema said.

"First she changed all the men into barking animals, and then when we complained that it wasn't fair and that we didn't want just women in our kingdom, she changed us too. She wouldn't let anyone challenge what she said," another one of the apes recounted as the wailing voices became louder.

Visibly moved by the woeful tale, Azashema put her arm around Momkey as tears streamed down the animal's face. "Please let us know if there is anything we can do to help you."

"You can't take the egg. We have to bring Azamerie back to life so she can change us back into women."

Momkey took them to her house, where, to their surprise, they saw many other houses in a town—so many houses, in fact, they couldn't remember where they had parked the Domionatic. *Azamerie's cruelty knows no bounds*, thought Michael as he looked at the row of houses stretching over the verdant field beyond his field of vision. The other apes dispersed to their houses.

"Please make yourselves comfortable and eat as much food as you want," Momkey said, bringing some apple pie and cheese to her kitchen table. They indulged in her offer until they were full.

"I knew this food was delicious when I first smelled it. How did you know we were hungry?" Lee asked, and everyone laughed.

"It was written all over your faces."

"Hate to break it to you, buddy, but we could hear your stomach complaining a mile away," Michael said as the girls chuckled.

"You apes are humans. What a surprise," Lee said, ignoring Michael's comment.

"Why do you want the egg?" Momkey asked.

Michael explained again, but this time he told her about his promise to Patrick and the men in the mountain.

"Patrick? Did you say Patrick?" Momkey asked excitedly. "One of the women in this town has a son by the name of Patrick! Please, tell me about him."

Azashema explained everything she knew about Patrick.

"Yes, he was blond," Momkey said. "He sounds like her son. Azamerie changed him, her husband, and my husband in the stadium before our eyes because they refused to listen to her, and then she vanished with them and all the men to a secret location. We looked for them for a long time, and we pleaded with her to tell us where they were, but she refused to tell us." Momkey wiped the tears from her eyes. "I have to wake her up so she can change us all back."

"Momkey, you don't have to wake her up," Joan said. "We can change you and the men back. Just show us where the egg is, and we will change you all back."

"How do you know you can change us back without Azamerie's magic powers?"

"Because we went to see the master of all magic and he gave us a special magic formula. We used it to change your men back into humans. If you just show us the egg, we promise to help you solve this problem too," Azashema told her, putting her hand on her shoulder.

"Follow me," Momkey said, heading toward the middle of the town. She opened a little door in one house in the row and asked them to follow her inside. In the house was a body lying on a bed surrounded by five elderly ape-women who treated the body's wounds with a natural remedy, a paste made of the green leaves they had picked from the forest mixed with some dry wood they had carefully ground into powder. They patted the medication all over the body.

"You go and take a look at that body and see if you recognize that person," Momkey said, moving closer to it.

As they moved closer, they realized with surprise it was the woman they thought they had killed. The apes were trying desperately to bring Azamerie back to life.

"How did you find her?" Lee asked.

"One day when we came back from hunting in the forest, we saw her lying by the roadside with blood all over her. One of the women took her in, brought her into this room, and called all the women she knew who could help heal her," one of the apes said.

"That same night I had a dream in which she told me how my people would enjoy the fruit of this land if she came back to life. She gave us good reasons why we should help her. When I woke up, I went to my grandmother, who is a magician and a dream interpreter. She told me it was a good dream, and that we should continue doing what we're doing and we wouldn't regret it. There are only a couple more hours left for us to use that egg on her body for her to fully recuperate. We'll celebrate that moment with singing and dancing, and you can be part of it," Momkey said delightedly.

Momkey thought for a moment and said, "Benta, these kids know Patrick."

"My boy Patrick?" Benta looked up in surprise.

"Yes," Michael began, "he's the leader of all the men."

"They always listened to him because he was a great magician," his mother said sadly, wiping her eyes. "Where is he? Please tell me where he is."

"In the gold mountain along with the other men," Michael told her.

"So that's where she put them," Benta said surprised. "And she probably made up that curse that you can't come close to the mountain or you'll get some disease—to scare us all away."

"Probably," Michael said.

"We have to wake her up so she'll change us back," Benta said with dark eyes looking sadly at Michael.

"If you wake Azamerie up, she will never change you back," Joan said. "All these years she refused to. What makes you think she will do it now?"

"Only we can change you back," Michael said, putting his hand on Benta's shoulder.

"But I don't even know who you are," she said, turning to her friend. "Do you know them, Momkey?"

"They're magicians. They said they have a magic formula from a master magician they can use to help the men, but they want the egg first."

"Do you want me to take you to see Patrick?" Michael suggested, hoping that he might convince her if she had the opportunity to see her son.

"Yes, yes, I want to see my boy."

"Then tell those apes to stop trying to heal Azamerie and to let us have her body. Tell them to go home. You and Momkey come with us and bring the egg. We will show you where Patrick and the men are."

Benta glanced at Momkey. "Okay, we'll come."

Momkey nodded and lifted up the egg from the stand above Azamerie's lifeless body. The other apes walked out toward their houses as Michael lifted Azamerie's body over his shoulder.

"We can't lose the egg, because the lives of all those thousands of men are wholly dependent on us," Lee said, looking at Momkey.

"I will give you the egg when I see Patrick," Benta said.

The Reunion

The group found the Domionatic and took off toward the mountain. When they entered, Michael put Azamerie's body on the floor, which was now searing hot. The rank odor forced Lee outside for fresh air.

"What is this machine? Doesn't look like a helicopter," Momkey said.

Lee covered his nose as his friends called him to get back inside. He went into the Domionatic and stood close to the door.

"We created this machine to get away from the Boscrollis," Michael answered.

"The Boscrollis? They are the meanest. They came to our town once and terrorized the women, so we put a curse on them and they can't enter our territory anymore," Benta said.

Michael started the motor, adjusted the controls, and pulled the lever that lifted the Domionatic into the air.

Afraid to fly over the Boscrollis' territory, Michael took a different route, flying southward and finally making a turn back to the west. After they landed only near the gold mountain site, the Domionatic began having technical difficulties, the engine refused to spark or restart. After many attempts, Michael was able to start the engine and tried to move it closer to the mountain, but it spouted smoke and he was afraid it would crash. They got out and started to walk. Fifteen minutes later, they found the ladder.

"Careful not to cut a piece of gold off the mountain. Although you don't get a disease if you touch it, everything vibrates and flashes if you cut a piece," Lee warned Momkey and Benta.

Michael tried to climb the ladder carrying Azamerie's body, but it was difficult. He tried again but couldn't. She was too heavy.

"Don't worry. My sister and I will carry her to the top," Joan told Michael.

Michael handed the body over to the girls, who each held one end and climbed the steps without difficulty. The girls never ceased to amaze Michael.

"We'll meet you at the mountaintop," said Azashema. Michael smiled up at them.

"Do you want us to carry the egg as well?" Joan asked.

"Don't worry about it, I will take it," Benta told her, taking it from Momkey.

Then, to Michael and Lee's surprise, the girls suddenly vanished.

"Ladies, you first," Michael said, and Momkey and Benta climbed the stairs one at a time.

"Are there lots of stairs?" Momkey asked.

"Yes." Michael answered, following Lee on the ladder. "I wanted to land the Domionatic closer, but it refused to start."

"Let me help you if you are tired," Lee said to Benta, who was holding the egg securely in her hand.

"I think I'm fine," Benta said, afraid of Lee's offer. Michael climbed slowly behind the women, until they finally reached the top. There, they spotted Joan and her sister sitting on the ground waiting, with Azamerie's body lying alongside them.

"Why did it take you so long?" she asked.

Michael was so tired. He leaned his back against the wall gasping for breath and was unable to answer her question.

"Are you all right, man?" Lee asked.

Michael glanced at him and said he was fine.

"Then let's get going, because as you can see, we're far behind schedule," Lee said.

"Now, what are we doing?" Azashema asked.

"We will do exactly as we were told by Marizama. Follow me," Michael said confidently.

"Marizama? The ghost? She knows everything, but I heard that it is scary to live with her," Momkey said.

Michael looked at her knowingly and said, "Uh huh." He turned and looked at his friends as if to say "I told you so." Lee carried Azamerie's body this time. Benta clutched the egg firmly. When they got to the door of the mountain where the men were, they saw the white horse on the loose, viciously trying to force its way into the room where the men were.

Some of the gold around the horse had already melted and was rolling into the room. The horse was crazily trotting back and forth, ready to destroy anything that came in its way. Michael told his friends to stop and keep silent.

"You wait here," he told everyone. "I'll go alone and talk to it."

"Are you crazy? Can't you see how scary it is?" Lee said.

"I know; that's why I am telling you to wait here."

"Why is that horse so fierce?" Benta asked, looking frightened at its aggressive trotting.

"It's a long story, Benta, but like you said, Marizama has all the answers and she told us how to handle it. So stay here with Lee, and I will be back soon to get you."

"I won't let you go alone; I'm coming with you," Lee insisted.

"No, you stay here and support Momkey and Benta. Only if you see that I'm in trouble then you should come to my rescue."

"Michael, please be careful," Azashema said, her voice resonating with concern.

Michael crept behind the thick wall of gold that separated the horse from them. Lee wasn't satisfied with Michael going alone, so he asked everyone to follow him. He and Joan took the body of Azamerie, and they carefully followed Michael, who didn't notice that they were trailing him stealthily.

As Michael moved nearer to the horse, he began to call it, his voice ringing out calmly into the quiet air. In response, the horse lifted its front legs high into the air. Michael yelled again, but the horse didn't react, so he touched it on its rear leg. The touch of Michael's hand provoked the horse to lash out with a fierce kick, walloping Michael into the gold wall. A little shaken but unfazed, he got up and screamed at the horse until it turned its head toward the impassioned voice.

When the horse saw Michael, it aimed its mighty legs high to smash him to the floor. It began to viciously step on top of Michael's shadow. Michael knew he was in danger. The horse was closing in on him. Michael found it difficult to move so he called

Lee for help. Lee was closer than Michael thought. Joan also came out from behind, surprising Michael.

"Deal with me!" she screamed at the horse. As she was calling, Lee and Azashema came out with the body of Azamerie and showed it to the horse.

"Here, take her and leave us alone!" Lee said.

The horse neighed loudly at them, raising its front legs higher in a menacing gesture.

"Now, we know how powerful you are, but I also know you can make yourself smaller. If you don't cooperate with us right now, we will have no choice but to kill you!" Azashema bellowed. Then, she quickly uncovered Azamerie's face for the horse to see.

In an instant, the horse transformed itself; it suddenly changed into a young and handsome boy close to their age. He had brown hair, dark brown eyes, a pointed nose, and a slim build. He stood before them cleanly dressed in a white suit. When he spoke, his voice sounded like thunder as lightning shoot from his mouth striking them. It threw them into the walls. Lee almost broke his neck, and their faces turned black with smoke.

The boy realized his voice was too strong and immediately corrected its volume. Michael and his friends sauntered back to him.

"What is your name?" Lee asked.

"My name is Cole. What are yours?"

Lee introduced himself and his friends.

"You're handsome-looking; are you really a man or a horse?" Michael asked.

"What's it to you?" Cole asked.

"Well, because we know Azamerie is a woman who changes people into different species to serve her purposes," Michael said.

"I'm a man," Cole answered. "Now what do you want? I am supposed to finish the job I am programmed to perform."

"What are you talking about? What kind of job are you programmed to do?" Michael demanded. "You think destroying the lives of innocent men in there is a job? You want to know what a real job is? A real job is to save lives, and that's what we're here to do."

He continued. "I know you're already programmed with great powers, and if we stand here searching for a solution until tomorrow, it won't make any sense to you. One thing I want you to remember is that you're a man and nothing is going to change that. All we're here to do is to make a deal with you. We will change you back into a man for good, send you back to your family, and give you the life you had before you were programmed to destroy yourself and others, if only you allow us to help save those men's lives in there," Michael offered.

Cole calmly and carefully listened to him as he closely studied everyone's movement. "You're right when you said that I won't understand what you are telling me. You think you're smart, but you're not. You are not trying to make a deal with me; you're trying to persuade me. I will take Azamerie from you without negotiation, and maybe you should listen to my instructions." Cole walked closer to the apes and looked in their eyes. "Do you know what you look like right now in front of me?"

Michael turned to look at his friends and answered, "No."

"You are like dead bodies!"

"What do you mean?" Lee asked.

"I mean that I can kill you right now just with my voice."

"Please don't say that, because you don't know us. We're great magicians, but we don't like to brag about our powers. Remember, we aren't here to fight; we are here to settle our differences peacefully and with respect. We know you're intelligent; that's why we're standing here negotiating with you." Michael knew that this was the only opportunity he had to end the battle without a fight. "Look! We have your queen, Azamerie. We know her powers are greater than yours, and she's in our hands. I'm not trying to threaten you, I'm only telling you the truth."

"You're not smarter than me!" Cole shot back, indignant. "I am smarter, stronger, more powerful, and more intelligent than any of you in this room! If you want a war, you have come to the right place, because I'm ready for battle! I will fight you until this mountain melts down, if that's what you want! Don't you know you are intruding in my house, and I control everything here?" Cole retorted with vengeance in his colored eyes.

"You are stupid," Joan roared. "If you were that smart, you would know that those men in there you are trying to kill might be your family members, as Benta here just found out. Her son Patrick is in there. We are trying to write Azamerie's wrong, and you are not letting us!"

"Accept our offer or leave now!" Michael warned.

At this bold ultimatum, Cole became furious and lashed out at Michael with his right fist. Knowing that Frank was working as his magical strength, Michael stood erect as Cole's five fingers broke one after another. Cole pulled his hand back and shook it vigorously until his fingers were repaired. He broke into mad laughter.

"Please don't test me. If you do, you're simply messing with fire," Michael warned him again.

"Okay. I think you have made a good offer, but first I would like to see the faces of all those men in that room, and then I will consider doing as you command," Cole said calmly.

Joan promptly jumped in to deny his request.

"I am not talking to you," Cole said rudely.

"You were programmed by a woman, and she's controlling you right now. You're a big fool!" She stared at him from his feet up to his face before stepping behind Michael.

"You know you have just made a big mistake by transforming yourself. You should have stayed as a horse; your power could still have been strong, but at this moment, you're no different from any ordinary kid walking out there in the city, not knowing what's ahead of him," Michael said.

"Why do you say that?" Cole asked.

"This is why!" With the information and help he was receiving from Frank, Michael immediately transmogrified him into an African bullfrog with a big chubby body. "You had enough time to think about either accepting our offer or dying."

Facing the Horse

"**I** don't think it was a good idea to change him into a frog and force him to change his mind," Azashema said in her usual gentle manner. "We will have to let him make his own decision. Whether he accepts ours or not, we must settle this matter peacefully."

"This guy is very dangerous. He was hypnotized by Azamerie, and unless he completes her dirty work, he won't rest," Michael told her.

"So what do you want to do with him now?" Lee asked.

"I know he can hear us, and I'm starting to have bad feelings about him. I think we should let him stay as a frog so we can think what to do next," Joan said.

"Maybe we should take him and keep him someplace safe before he disappears," Lee suggested.

"Let's sit right here and think for few minutes, because we can't make any mistakes that might take us all the way back to the beginning. We have Azamerie, the egg, and the horse," Michael said, sitting on the ground near the frog.

"Wait a minute. Let me talk to him," Momkey suddenly said. "Turn him back into a man."

After Michael changed Cole back into a young man, Momkey knelt before him and looked deeply into his eyes, saying, "You are a beautiful young man."

Cole looked down at the ground.

"I bet your mom misses you very much. You might not remember that several years ago the men of Texdulonicram had a standoff with Azamerie. You might have been a little boy when we all sat at the stadium and Azamerie insisted she would add 100 percent tax to everything we bought, so that she could build herself a palace. And you may not remember the moment she changed all the men into beasts and then vanished with them." Momkey looked at him closely. "But I remember."

Cole avoided her gaze.

"You see, I lost my young son and husband."

Cole looked up. "Why ..."

"Do I look the way I do?" Momkey completed his train of thought. "When Azamerie came back to the stadium alone without the men, the women began the fight of their lives. They screamed, cried, and pleaded with her to bring the men back, but she refused. That is when we came charging at her with whatever we had." Momkey began to cry. "She changed us into apes and took away our lives."

"We endangered our lives to help the men and women of Texdulonicram get their lives back. We don't know you, but one thing we do know is that you have the right to live your own life, and that's why we're here," Michael said.

"Remember one thing: we're here to execute our promise to the men in there; but if you think we're evil like Azamerie, just say so and we'll leave this room and you'll never see us again," Lee added.

"You *are* evil," Cole roared and, without warning, changed back into a horse. He lifted his powerful front legs toward them. In a flash, Michael changed him back into a frog. Joan quickly grabbed the frog and roped the legs. Lee suggested they consult Marizama for advice about the situation.

"I was just thinking the same thing," Joan said.

"Let me see if I can call her." Michael called her name five times, and she appeared. Michael explained the situation and then told her about Momkey and Benta.

"I was wondering why it took you so long to contact me. Did you see the rope that was attached to the horse?"

"No. We only saw the horse all by itself," Michael answered.

"You must go through that door right now because that rope has transmogrified into a wild dragon snake, and it's trying to force its way into the main room to consume the men alive. Be very careful, because it's viciously dangerous."

"It will be difficult to kill that big snake you're talking about without a major fight, and we're tired of fighting," Michael said.

"If you do not choose that, then you must take the body of Azamerie and the frog back to the mountaintop; you must not go close to the ladder from where you came, but to the other side of the mountain. Lay the body of Azamerie on the far right end. Tie the frog's legs so it won't jump away. Lay it on the floor far to the left.

"One of you should take the egg, stand in the middle, and hold it firmly toward the sun with both hands. No matter what happens, don't drop that egg. Another one of you should stand firmly behind the frog and another behind Azamerie; the others should stand right behind the one holding the egg. In this case, I would suggest the females do that.

"Something will happen, I don't know what, but you will have to wait until it's completely done; then you will see what will happen next. From there, you can call me."

"We've got to go." Michael told the girls to follow with the egg and the frog while he and Lee carried the body of Azamerie. They quickly positioned themselves and prepared to go.

Final Preparation

"**A**re you waiting for my command? Let's go!" Michael said with a half-grin. He and Lee sauntered to the front of the group. Then he and Lee veered around the mountaintop and selected a good position as Marizama had instructed. They relished the moment, cupping their hands over their eyes and looking at the city below and off to the distance where Momkey's community lay.

"Who's going to hold up the egg?" Michael asked looking at the girls.

"Why are you staring at us?" Azashema asked.

"Because Marizama said a female should do this. You were there and you heard her, that's why."

"I'll do it." Azashema took the egg from him.

"I'll stand right behind you and hold you just in case anything goes wrong," Michael said with an obvious smile.

"You won't stand behind me, only my sister will," Azashema said.

"Are you afraid I might touch you?"

"Listen, Michael, we have no time for questions; we must do this job now and get it over with. Can't you just imagine what those men under there are going through at this moment?" Joan said, siding with her sister. "We're risking our lives for them, not because we're in love with you. Now if you don't mind, I advise you to go do your job and let us do ours."

Michael blushed and glanced at Lee, but Lee looked away, embarrassed for his friend. Michael shamefacedly ambled away and stood behind Azamerie's body, while Lee quietly went and stood behind the frog.

"Why did you do that? You were rude and you embarrassed me," Azashema said to her sister.

"They must understand their boundaries so we can work in peace."

"I think Michael is a charming, strong young man, and I kind of like him," Azashema said.

"If I ever hear you say that again, I will disintegrate your teeth! Never, ever say that around me again," Joan said in her usual no-nonsense voice. "Ask them if they're ready before we start."

Joan held the egg firmly erect toward the sun for about twenty minutes but nothing happened.

"Give it to me. Let me try," Azashema said. She took her sister's position. Michael and Lee, meanwhile, remained in their positions, afraid to begin a confrontation with the girls.

Azashema glanced at her sister and grinned. She turned and held up the egg firmly toward the sun, and in less than two minutes, a red light, like an otherworldly floating rope, shot from the sky. The light suddenly circled them and more bright lights followed. It was so bright that Michael couldn't see anything. Powerful waves of heat were emitted by the blinding light.

Azashema moved closer and clasped her sister firmly for more balance. Some of the light entered the egg. It shone for an hour before it suddenly disappeared from the egg.

"The egg is empty!" Azashema told her sister, but at that moment, her sister was staring at her in an unusual manner with her mouth open.

"What is happening to you?" Joan asked her.

"What are you talking about?" she said in a sweet voice with tears rolling down her face. "I mean you've become prettier. I hardly recognize you anymore."

"I'm feeling so good, like I could move this mountain. I have never felt this way!"

When Joan moved closer to Azashema, her beauty brightened as well. She hugged her sister and told her how blissful she too had become. "We're going to cherish this moment!"

Michael was wrestling hard with Azamerie who had suddenly spring to life, and Lee was nowhere in sight. The frog had grown fatter and bigger like a balloon and was sitting upright glaring at them.

"I think they're in trouble," Azashema yelled out. "You go find Lee, and I will see what is happening with Michael!" They quickly separated and ran in different directions.

Azashema saw with horror that Azamerie had come to life and was trying to regenerate. Michael wrestled and struggled to pull his legs out from Azamerie's mouth as she was trying to swallow him.

"Do something before she swallows me!" Michael cried out.

"I knew this woman would carry out her same cruel behavior no matter what, but I will tell you one thing, Azamerie: me and my sister will be some of the last people you will see on the face of this gold mountain!" she yelled madly.

Azamerie just glared at her as she fought harder to swallow Michael. He was crying out louder and louder. As his legs pushed down her stomach, he felt as if he was entering a crushing machine.

Joan heard her sister and then lifted the empty eggshell. She threw it at Azamerie's head, and it shattered into tiny fragments. Then, suddenly, as if she had swallowed a grenade, Azamerie's body exploded. Michael was thrown to the edge of the mountain, but as he plummeted down, he managed to grab on to a little piece of gold that jutted out hundreds of feet above the ground.

"Help!" he cried.

"Hang on! Try not to wobble too much! Clutch that gold with one hand and give me your other hand!" Joan said.

Michael struggled to extend his left hand toward her, but the piece of gold began to crack under his weight, causing him to fall a few inches lower. As it was about to break off completely, he let out a large shriek. Luckily, Joan managed to grab his hand and forcefully pull him up. He was soaked with Azamerie's blood. He lay still on the mountaintop taking in gulps of air.

"Are you all right?" Azashema asked.

"Yes," he managed to say. "You saved my life again."

"What happened?" Joan wanted to know.

"When the bright light overshadowed me, I was completely dazzled. After a couple of minutes, I felt my legs entering down a slippery tube. I guess when my eyes were closed; she took advantage of the opportunity and tried to swallow me."

"She never gives up," Joan said. "Can you get up? We have to go find the others."

Michael rose slowly and they ran to where they thought Lee was. When they got there, they called Lee's name, and Momkey and Benta answered from far behind the frog. They found them standing, staring at Lee's face and trying to convince the frog to let Lee go.

"What happened?" Michael asked.

"The frog is sitting on him, and it is difficult for him to breathe. I've tried to push the frog's belly away from his face but it's too heavy," Momkey told them.

"Do you still have the eggshell?" Azashema asked her sister.

"I used all of it to save Michael," Joan replied. "It all happened too fast."

Michael ran to the front to face the frog. "Let my brother go now before you die like Azamerie!" He began poking its face to gain its attention. "We can help you. I know you're confused in there, but we will find a way to bring you back to your real self for good," Michael told the frog. "You're sitting on top of my brother, and he's not breathing. Shove forward a little so I can yank him out."

Joan and her sister were trying to pull Lee by the hands, but the harder they tried, the harder Lee screamed from the excruciating pain, so they left him alone. Michael told everyone to help push the frog off Lee. He tapped the frog three times, signaling him that they were ready to smash into him. As the frog struggled to lift itself, it suddenly pushed its legs backward, slamming all three of them back into the wall of the mountain. Meanwhile, Momkey and Benta kept patting the top of his head and talking to him softly, reminding him that he was Cole, the boy whose life was ruined by Azamerie. The frog finally managed to remove itself from Lee, but Lee immediately collapsed in an unconscious heap. Michael and the girls lifted him and held him sitting erect until he came to himself.

"How on earth did this happen?" Joan asked.

"When my eyes were closed from the strong bright light, the frog leaped at me and knocked me down. He sat on me and tried to kill me by squeezing my face," Lee explained.

"So, what are we going to do with the frog?" Azashema asked.

"I want to turn it back into a human," Michael said.

"I think it may become too dangerous. I think we should at least make it smaller so we can have more control over it," Lee suggested.

"We will make the frog smaller," agreed Azashema. "Now I would like you to move back and give us some room so we can work comfortably."

Michael and Lee watched as the girls changed the frog to normal size, allowing Michael to tie its legs.

"What will we do with that mighty snake that's after the men?" Joan reminded them.

"I don't know until we get there," Michael said.

"We have to do something to save Patrick and his men," Benta said, and Momkey patted her shoulder in an attempt to comfort her. They walked quickly back to the opening of the mountain to rejoin the men and saw the snake's head already inside the room. Its slithery green skin was dotted with dark brown spots, and its tail was nearly the length of the room. It moved from side to side, almost hitting Michael. Frightened screaming emerged from inside the room.

"Hope we're not too late. We have to hurry and do something," Lee said.

The girls ran to attack the snake from the back. They tried to cut off its tail, because they knew it would be difficult to yank its head out of the room; it was too large. Azashema and Joan stood at either end of the room. As the snake's tail came toward Azashema, Joan released the force in her finger to pin the snake's tail against the wall where Azashema stood. She quickly tied the tail into a knot. Provoked by unexpected pain, the snake released a thick, dark red fire into the room, stirring a deep-seated fear in Michael.

"Keep on going. You're doing a good job. Don't stop!" Michael screamed as he and Lee rushed to help, leaving the frog in the corner with Momkey and Benta. Michael didn't realize Frank had been secretly following him, but then he heard Frank calling him. Michael turned to look at his right shoulder.

Frank gave Michael a couple of long sharp knives. "You must crawl under it and make sure you tear its throat. Then it will be helpless. Do it fast. One last thing: do not leave this frog alone."

Michael and Lee did as they were instructed. Soon, the giant snake began to wrestle for its life. It was crying and whacking everything around it as it tried to haul its ugly head and long sharp horns out of the door. By the time it got out through the doorway, the girls had already reduced it to feebleness by separating its legs, and Michael began to frantically tear at its throat. When the snake finally died, its body erupted in flames and burned away, leaving a copious amount of fetid black ash.

Michael and his friends rejoiced. Joan ran into the room where the men were to see what had happened.

"The room is hollow and roasting," she told Benta and Momkey after she ran outside, frightened. They all rushed into the room to see for themselves. When they saw the vacant, ash-filled room, they placed their hands on their heads tearfully, fearing the snake had consumed all the men.

Lee and Benta, not giving up, began yelling out, "Patrick! Patrick!"

"Wherever you are, please come out," Benta said with a hopeful voice.

"It's us," Lee said. "We've killed the snake, and the way is now clear. We're here to take you home just like we promised!" Lee's voice echoed back to him.

Michael sat confused, thinking how their hard efforts had been wasted in vain. He looked at the frog and said, "At least one of the men survived. But look, this room is clean, just the way it was when we first slipped in here. Something isn't right. I think they're hiding someplace fearing for their lives. They are too smart to just let that beast kill them."

"Remember we're dealing with higher magic powers. With magic, unexpected things do happen. We should be thinking like magicians," Azashema said.

"What will we say to the people in town? They'll still be waiting for us to deliver their leader. If these men were here, we would have had a good excuse. I don't know why, but I still have the feeling they are here hiding somewhere. You guys should watch this frog; I will search around," Michael said, standing up and walking toward the second door.

"We'll wait here; if you encounter any problems just scream our names. Make sure you don't go too far," Lee cautioned.

"Guys, stop being indolent! Get up. Let's help him, I think he knows what he's talking about, and we must show him we support him. He's not losing hope like we are," Joan said.

"You are right." They got up.

"Don't forget the frog," Michael reminded.

Lee took the frog and tailed them, with Benta and Momkey following. They trekked deeper into the mountain as they called Patrick's name, trying to summon him from the unknown place he waited for them.

Michael ambled straight down toward a tiny statue where he thought he heard voices whispering. When he searched behind the wall, he saw shadows moving and thought there might be something there. He walked over with caution to investigate. To his surprise, he stumbled across the entire group sitting there, terrified. They were all crammed on top of each other just to fit into the small quarters. Michael called his friends and asked them to peek behind the wall. Benta breathed a loud sigh of relief.

"Come out, you are safe. There's nothing here to worry about anymore," Joan said as they helped the men out of the small quarters.

Patrick explained how the beast had consumed a few of them.

"You all will have a lot to explain to us once we get out of here safely. We don't need to squander anymore time. We will get you out of here as quickly as possible," Azashema assured them. They had no choice but to agree with her. Many of the men were wide-eyed and looking around fearfully, praying that this would be the end of their suffering.

"Okay, people. Let's get out of here quickly," Azashema said.

Changes

"There are no words I can use to describe our gratitude," Patrick said, embracing Michael.

"That's my boy!" Tears escaped rapidly from Benta's eyes. She walked toward Patrick who backed away.

"Get that ape away from me," he told Michael.

"Patrick, it's me," Benta said, unable to control the wailing that now came loudly from her throat. "I missed you so much."

"What's going on here?" Dogsen asked Patrick, who looked at him in confusion.

"Patrick," Michael began, "you men are not the only ones who were changed into animals. Apparently, after Azamerie changed you, she also changed a group of women who came to fight her to get the men back."

"If she had it her way, no one in Texdulonicram would have any free will. Everything had to be done her way," Momkey said.

"Patrick, Benta is your mother," Michael said.

Patrick walked closer to Benta and looked into her moist eyes. Benta flung her arms around him and he tightened up.

"We'll change her back soon," Joan said, reassuring Patrick, whose anxiety was painfully visible across his visage. "You must listen to us now. When you're out there, you can do whatever you want. Are you all with me?" Michael asked.

"We're ready," Patrick answered alone.

"No, I want to hear all of you together. I'll ask again. Are you all ready to go home?" Michael yelled so that the men in the back of the room could hear him.

"Yes, we are ready!" they answered zealously.

"Then follow us."

Benta and Patrick walked behind Michael. Lee, Momkey, and the girls walked behind them. Michael waited for a few minutes before motioning to the men to proceed to the door. They followed him with confidence, but as they came nearer to the outside door, they stopped.

Michael only realized it after he had gone forward. He walked back toward them. "What's the problem?"

"Our problem is that door," Patrick said. "I mean, would it be wise if one or two of us walked through to see what happens?" Patrick suggested.

"There's nothing to worry about," Michael said, but Patrick didn't look convinced.

Lee and the others were already sitting outside exhausted, leaving Michael with the headache.

"Now who will walk out with me first?" he asked.

"In this case, we will have to find a volunteer," Patrick said.

"Okay, hurry up!" Michael was becoming impatient.

Patrick asked the group of men to volunteer, but no one came forward.

"You will have to do this yourself this time," Michael said.

"What do you want me to do?" Patrick asked fearfully.

"You must hold yourself like a leader and do it first, because we can't stand here all day," Michael said impatiently.

The men looked around and shuffled their feet. After a few moments, two older men in their late sixties walked up to Michael and volunteered to take the risk.

"What are your names, gentlemen?"

"My name is Vetrgote, and he is Zacreftregen."

"Okay then, follow me."

The other men moved back with fear, watching the two volunteers. When Vetrgote and Zacreftregen got to the door and stepped out with one foot, two dark black shadows in human form flew from above the door and hit them with force in their stomachs. The two men flew back inside the room. They lay on the floor screaming and writhing in pain.

Michael was surprised. He thought the ritual Marizama had set out for them was complete. He wondered what went wrong.

"You have come to kill us, haven't you?" Patrick was furious. "You are liars, and we don't want anything to do with you anymore!"

"I think that what just happened is beyond our control," Lee told Patrick, coming in from outside with the group following him. He turned toward Michael. "I suggest we call Marizama again."

"You call her," Azashema told him.

He did, and Marizama appeared. They told her what was happening. Without thinking, she ordered them to behead the frog.

"Why do you want us to do that? We have seen him as a human, and he's an attractive young man who we believe was transformed by Azamerie to carry out her dirty task. We believe we can save him," Michael said.

"Stop talking and do something quickly!" Marizama cried.

Lee hit the frog hard, and it fell to the solid floor. It attempted to get up and jump away, but Joan pursued it and, wielding one of the knives she used on the snake, chopped off its head in one swift, brutal stroke. She walked over to the bloody body to make sure it was dead. Then she went back to where Marizama appeared on the wall and told her.

"You're all a bunch of fakes, including Benta there who says she's my mother. I urge you to get out of here before I have my men after you!" Patrick said.

"Patrick, I'm not a fake! I fought Azamerie with all I had to see you and your dad again," Benta said.

"Shhh, Marizama is still giving us instructions," Joan said.

"Take the dead frog and keep it. I will tell you what to do with it later." Then she called them together to whisper some more advice so they wouldn't make any mistakes. "You see, the task is already accomplished. The only thing left to do is to take the frog into the room and rub its blood on each and every man's forehead before letting them out. I know that this time it will be difficult for them to believe your words, but you'll have to convince them, because that is the only way out." Marizama looked at Michael. "By the way, the people of this city have clustered together at the city square and are awaiting your decision. They now believe Azamerie is dead. You guys should hurry and get out of there. Use force if necessary."

"When we are done, what do you want us to do with the head of the frog and its body?" Michael asked.

"Nothing, all you have to do is keep it. When you come, you will see for yourself what will happen."

"Thank you so much, Marizama. We'll be seeing you soon," Michael told her.

"If something goes wrong this time, I won't be able to help you. I don't think you should panic," Marizama said. They wished her good-bye, and she left.

"Come on, what are you waiting for? Didn't you hear what she said?" Michael said walking toward the men, with his friends in tow. Everyone glared at them ravenously, as if they wanted to eat them alive, and several of them shivered at the thought.

"I know you all are intelligent men, but sometimes there are things you have to consider doing, no matter how clever you are. Remember, we are human and bound to make mistakes.

"I want to say thanks for trusting us in the first place. That trust brought you back to being human again. I believe that somewhere in your heart, you still have trust in us. You know that we would not have made you human had we any intention to harm you. We are almost at the end of this ordeal. We want to get you out of here, and we don't want any more men hurt.

"I told you some time ago that there are many things you will have to withstand in order to live. Thank you for listening to me once more. I'm sure that when we get out of this hellhole, you will have a whole new life ahead of you. My friends and I are open to any questions you may want to ask," Michael said.

Zacreftregen, who was lying down in front of Michael, asked in a pained voice, "So what do you want us to do?"

Wiltrofloyen quickly cut Michael short from answering. "We didn't really understand what you just said. Just some fancy words to con us—looks like to me."

"I can see you are irate, but I would advise you and everyone in this room to calm down. We're not fighting here. Now to cut this matter short and get us all out of here quickly, we will rub a little of this blood on your foreheads, and you will walk right through that door."

Patrick ambled to the front and stared rudely into Michael's eyes. "Do you think we're animals? I've listened to you carefully, and I know you are struggling to complete the job Azamerie wanted done. We all are sick and tired of your lies. We'll stay in here and die with dignity!

"Look around you. You're dealing with human beings; human beings just like you! Do you know how many of us have died since you came here? Even though we were Vasferes, we didn't know anything different and we were happy; we accepted our situation and decided to live with it until you and your friends showed up!" Patrick was outraged; he was speaking so loudly that his saliva flew toward Michael's face.

"Stop talking to him like that! Do you know who he is? You can't talk like that to a person who has striven to make you men and give you back your lives—who do you think you are?" Lee said boldly, surprising Michael. "I will tell you one thing, and I want you all to listen to me for your own sake. We will rub this blood on your foreheads and will walk you out one at a time. We won't negotiate with you anymore, and this time, our word is law!"

"It's amazing to see that you feel you have so much power to rule our lives. Who do you think you are?" Patrick retorted.

Zacreftregen went up to Lee and said, "Please rub the blood on my forehead and take me outside because I don't want to die in here." He was shivering and tears were rolling down his checks.

"Shame on you all, how could you let this old man be braver than you young, strong men?" Joan said.

"Open your eyes, little woman! Can't you see he's old and about to die?" Dogsen said.

"Okay, because of your answer, I will make sure this old man lives longer than you," she said.

"Oh yeah, if you want to use your magic and kill me before killing all the others, you're welcome to try," he laughed mockingly.

Undeterred by his hubristic challenge, Joan used her magic to subdue him into an example of the power she wielded. He toppled over and fell to the ground.

"I know you are scared, and that's why you should have kept your mouth shut. If I were you, I'd start rejoicing because you're going home; you will never have to remember this gold mountain again," she told him.

She rubbed the blood on his forehead and asked Michael and Lee to do the same to Zacreftregen. They complied, and then led the two men outside the door. Joan stayed back with the other men. She warned the others to stay right where they were.

"Wait a minute, are you trying to imprison us?" Patrick asked fearlessly.

"You ask too many questions," came the sharp retort from Joan. "Keep your mouth shut, because you will be the next person to walk out that door with me!"

"Patrick has always been a willful boy; strong, and everyone followed him. Had a hard time being led around though," said Benta.

"Shut up, stupid woman," Patrick said. At that moment, Joan turned Benta into her human form. She was a fair-skinned and petite woman who appeared to be scared of her son.

"It *is* you," Patrick said. At that moment, his face dropped with shame, and he looked pitiful.

He watched Michael and Lee carry Zacreftregen and Dogsen through the door. When both men made it outside, some of those inside began to cheer, clapping their hands happily.

Michael was surprised to see Zacreftregen walk without assistance after he had made it outside. "I thought your hip was broken."

"Yes, it was, but as I was passing through that door, I felt something strike me on my hip. It hurt. As soon as I stepped out here, all the pain vanished. It feels great. Now I can remember everything that happened just like it was yesterday," he said with great joy.

Even though they saw what was happening, some of the men still weren't convinced. They were whispering to each other that Michael was setting up a death trap.

Michael warned those who made it out to stay outside; it was a mistake to try going back into the room. When Michael glanced at them, he knew they were so overexcited that they might slip into the room unknowingly. He asked Lee to watch them.

Michael went back inside, rubbed the blood on a couple of men's foreheads and walked them outside. The blood left thick red smears on their flesh. Joan clutched Patrick by the hand as he struggled to escape the blood ritual, but she managed to hold him down and forced him outside. Soon, all of the men were out successfully.

In a joyous display of mutual affection, the men were singing and dancing their traditional song, holding hands in circles. After, they embraced each other, telling their friends they loved them.

Michael started thinking about how he would to get the men to the ground safely.

"All right, people! I want you to follow us; try to be careful when you are climbing up the stairs to the mountaintop!" Michael warned.

"Mountaintop? What are we going to do at the mountaintop?" Patrick asked.

"Good question. That's where the ladders are to take us down to the ground," he answered.

"How far it is from here?" Dogsen asked.

"Not too far. We can make it in two hours," Michael answered calmly.

"Fellows, these children have done a lot for us, and yet each time they say something, you question their judgment. That isn't right. We should give them the credit they deserve so we can get out of here quickly," Benta said.

Patrick walked over to Michael. "I'm ready to follow you, whichever way you want to take me."

"Thank you for your cooperation; we won't disappoint you," Michael said as Benta held her son's arm and they walked behind him.

"Okay, people, if you're ready then follow us!" Joan said as she ambled to the front.

All of the men followed. At the mountaintop, the men were able to see the light of day and felt something they hadn't felt in a long time: freedom. They hungrily inhaled the fresh, pure air and relished the ineffable beauty of the city lights all around them.

Michael showed Patrick the side of the mountain where the ladders were. He and Lee stayed up with one group; Joan and her sister went down with the other group of men to make sure they were all safe.

"Will you change me back into a human?" Momkey asked on the mountaintop.

"Sure," Michael promised. "Just as soon as we get down the ladder." He turned to Lee to make sure he had the frog, and then waited patiently until the last man went down the ladder before putting his foot on the first rung to make his way down.

When the whole group touched the ground safely, the men were singing and dancing their traditional song, holding hands in circles and some fell to their knees to kiss the ground in exuberant gratitude.

GREAT BOOKS, GREAT SAVING!

Kindle Version of TOWN TRAP is available on amazon.com

You Can Save Money Off The Retail Price Of Any Book You Purchase From JD BOOKS!

Email JD Publishing Company Today To Start Saving!
jdpublishingcompany@yahoo.ca

All Orders Are Subject To Availability.
Shipping and Handling Charges Apply.
Offers and Prices Subject To Change Without Notice.

www.ingramcontent.com/pod-product-compliance
Lightning Source LLC
Chambersburg PA
CBHW070038260626
47159CB00005B/2075